Michael Underwood and The Murder Room

>>> This title is part of The Murder Room, our series dedicated to making available out-of-print or hard-to-find titles by classic crime writers.

Crime fiction has always held up a mirror to society. The Victorians were fascinated by sensational murder and the emerging science of detection; now we are obsessed with the forensic detail of violent death. And no other genre has so captivated and enthralled readers.

Vast troves of classic crime writing have for a long time been unavailable to all but the most dedicated frequenters of second-hand bookshops. The advent of digital publishing means that we are now able to bring you the backlists of a huge range of titles by classic and contemporary crime writers, some of which have been out of print for decades.

From the genteel amateur private eyes of the Golden Age and the femmes fatales of pulp fiction, to the morally ambiguous hard-boiled detectives of mid twentieth-century America and their descendants who walk our twenty-first century streets, The Murder Room has it all. >>>

The Murder Room
Where Criminal Minds Meet

themurderroom.com

T0352442

Michael Underwood (1916–1992)
Michael Underwood (the pseudonym of John Michael Evelyn) was born in Worthing, Sussex and educated at Christ Church College, Oxford. He was called to the Bar in 1939 and served in the British army during World War Two. He returned to work in the Department of Public Prosecutions until his retirement in 1976, and wrote almost 50 crime novels informed by his career in the law. His five series characters include Sergeant Nick Atwell and lawyer Rosa Epton, of whom is was said by the *Washington Post* that she 'outdoes Perry Mason'.

By the same author

Simon Manton
Murder on Trial (1958)
Murder Somewhere Else (1958)
Death on Remand (1959)
False Witness (1959)
Death in Camera (1959)
Arm of the Law (1959)
Crime upon Crime (1960)
Death by Misadventure (1960)
Adam's Case (1961)
They Love not Poison (19..)
(19..)
Out Goeth Not (1965)
The Genial Stranger (19..)
The Vanishing Conspirator (19..)

Nicolas Hilary
The Man Who Died on Friday (1967)
The Man Who Killed Too Soon (1968)

Martin Ainsworth
The Shadow Game (1969)
Trout in the Milk (1971)
Reward for a Defector (1973)
The Anxious Conspirator (1972)

Ross Jeron
A Picture of Death (1980)
Circle upon Circle (1980)
Double Jeopardy (1981)

(Order of Death (1983)
A Party to Murder (1983)
Death in Camera (1984)
The Unknown Man (1983)
Death of a Friend
Gallows (1959)
The Juror (1987)
The Last of the Crime (1981)
(19..) August 1981
Appealing Cases (19..)
A Dangerous Business (1991)
Rose's Dilemma (1990)
The Seeds of Murder (1991)
Guilty Conscience (1992)

Mark Aitch
The Juror (1975)
Menaces, Menaces (1976)
The Fatal Trip (1977)
Murder with Malice (1977)
Crime Above (1976)

Standing trial
A Crime Apart (1966)
Shem's Demise (1970)
The Silent Liars (1970)
Anything but the Truth (1976)
Suspect of Justice (1978)
Verdict of Circumstance (1979)
A Glass of Death (1980)
Hand of Fate (1981)

Menaces, Menaces

Michael Underwood

An Orion book

Copyright © Isobel Mackenzie 1966

The right of Michael Underwood to be identified as the author of this work has been asserted in accordance with the Copyright, Designs and Patents Act 1988.

This edition published by
The Orion Publishing Group Ltd
Orion House
5 Upper St Martin's Lane
London WC2H 9EA

An Hachette UK company
A CIP catalogue record for this book is available from the British Library

ISBN 978 1 4719 0798 2

www.orionbooks.co.uk

CHAPTER ONE

He was five feet eight inches tall, round-faced and sallow-cheeked. He wore his hair, which was black, slicked back and parted on the left side with mathematical precision, so that the top of his head reminded one of an advertisement for a popular hair-cream. He was forty-two years old and his name was Herbert Sipson.

He now looked about him with the mildly anxious air of a late arrival at a cocktail party searching for a familiar face. It was as though he was not quite sure whether he would recognise his host.

His eyes swiftly took in the whole scene before his gaze settled on Mr Justice Tidyman who sat staring back at him across the short divide separating dock and bench.

He gave the judge a small, almost apologetic, bow. Apologetic, perhaps, because he was the last arrival, though that was hardly his fault, but, more likely, because his whole life was a sort of apology. A seeming apology for putting others to trouble. And there could be no doubt that to have become the object of a criminal trial at the Old Bailey was causing a lot of trouble to a lot of people, albeit well-paid trouble to the regular participants in such dramas.

The judge made no acknowledgement of Herbert's small, polite bow and his expression of judicial detachment gave no hint of what was passing through his mind as Herbert stood at the front of the dock and glanced shyly about him.

'Looks just what his record shows him to be, a dangerous and unscrupulous blackmailer. Hope the jury will recognise it, too, without the benefit of knowing his record.' So ran the judge's thoughts as the Clerk of the Court rose and turned round to speak to him. He leaned forward with frowning reluctance to catch the clerk's whispered words, then with unchanged expression motioned him peremptorily to sit down again.

The clerk cast prosecuting counsel a glance inviting sympathy for being the most misunderstood man in Court, but counsel anticipated the move and averted his gaze. Anyone who knew Tidyman was aware that you didn't speak until you were spoken to. But one or two of the newer clerks seemed to interpret their role as judge's confidant and friend. Well, this one had learnt his lesson for the day.

The judge now spoke.

'Mr Sipson,' – although one of the old school, Mr Justice Tidyman was well aware that if you addressed an accused these days without the prefix of Mr, you risked antagonising some of the jury, who had become increasingly sensitive about these things. There were invariably one or two jurors who identified themselves with the accused rather than with those ranged against him – 'I understand that you are not legally represented.'

'That is so, my lord,' Herbert said with a small, ingratiating smile. 'I was offered legal aid by the magistrate but I declined the offer. Though, of course, I was very grateful to him.'

'Be that as it may,' the judge remarked, swallowing his even stronger feeling of dislike of Herbert now that he had spoken, 'it is not too late for you to change your mind, though it would mean putting your case back for a short time while Counsel familiarised himself with the details. You are facing extremely grave charges and I am sure that it would assist the Court, as well as being in your own interest, if your defence were to be conducted by experienced counsel. In these circumstances, you may like to reconsider your position and to make an application which I would certainly see fit to grant.'

While the judge was speaking, Herbert had taken a grip on the front of the dock as though to frustrate a possible attempt to remove him by force. The judge had scarcely finished when he said, 'I am most grateful to your lordship, but I would still prefer to defend myself on these charges. Moreover, I am heartened by the knowledge that I shall receive the fairest possible trial at your lordship's hands. I assure your lordship that I will endeavour not to waste the Court's time, which would certainly be the case if I accepted your lordship's kind offer at this late stage.'

The words were accompanied by a look which seemed to ask the judge for forgiveness for such temerity. For his part, Mr Justice Tidyman, who had spent a lifetime playing forensic poker, gave nothing away by his expression, but each word seemed to have an icicle attached to it as he said, 'So be it.'

Nevertheless, Herbert gave him a further small bow.

'Arraign him, then,' Mr Justice Tidyman added testily when the silence which followed began to become obvious.

The clerk who was still in a state of simmering dudgeon rose and addressed Herbert.

'There are two counts in the indictment against you. The first alleges that on the 8th of November with a view to gain for yourself in a letter addressed to the managing director of the Shangri-La Bingo Company Limited you made an unwarranted demand for £10,000 with menaces. The second count alleges that on the 6th of November without lawful excuse you damaged the premises of the Shangri-La Bingo Company Limited in Perkin Street, Putney, intending to damage such property or being reckless as to whether such property would be damaged.' He looked up from the document he had been reading. 'To the first count, do you plead guilty or not guilty?'

Herbert who had been listening with an expression of mild reproach now said, 'I plead not guilty to both counts. I am completely innocent of these charges.' And he gave the jurors who were waiting to be sworn a small wistful smile. Not your fault and not mine that we've been dragged together into this legal tarradiddle, it seemed to say.

It was at this point that Detective Sergeant Nick Attwell whispered something to Detective Chief Superintendent

Lapham, the officer in charge of the case, and slipped out of Court, avoiding Herbert's interested glance as he did so. He could hardly inform the accused that he was only going to phone his pregnant wife. Indeed, he hadn't even mentioned this to his guvnor, muttering only that he was going out to make sure all the witnesses had arrived. He would do that, anyway, on his return to Court.

Clare Attwell was in the process of shifting a piece of furniture when the telephone rang. She guessed it was probably her husband. He was liable to ring at all hours to make sure she was all right, even though the baby was not expected for another month.

'It's me, darling. Everything all right?'

'As fine as when you left me a couple of hours ago,' Clare said lightly. 'Where are you speaking from?'

'The Old Bailey. The trial's just starting.'

'A fight, is it?'

'You bet. Our Herbert has never pleaded guilty to anything in his life. And this time, he's defending himself, which has made the judge livid, so that's all to the good.'

'He should make the *Guinness Book of Records* as the most persistently unsuccessful blackmailer history has ever known.'

Nick laughed. It was nice being married to someone who could talk his shop, particularly as Clare obviously had no regrets at having exchanged the duties of Woman Detective Constable Reynolds for those of Mrs Nick Attwell.

'What were you doing when I phoned?' Nick enquired, a faint note of suspicion in his voice.

'Resting on the sofa with my feet up,' Clare replied without a tremor.

'Good. Make sure you don't overdo things, darling. I must get back into Court. See you this evening, though I'll call you again before then.'

Clare replaced the receiver with a smile and returned to the piece of furniture she was moving.

By the time Nick got back into Court, the jury of eight women and four men had been sworn and Philip Vane was about to open the case for the prosecution.

'Have you ever seen such a jury?' Detective Chief Super-intendent Lapham muttered to Nick as he sat down. 'They look like rejects from all the other courts.'

'Pity most of the women are such middle-aged types,' Nick murmured back, glancing across to where the jury sat. 'Herbert'll play up boyish injured innocence for all he's worth.'

'He's already begun.' Lapham shook his head disbelievingly. 'But he can't get away with it! Not Herbert Sipson!'

They lapsed into silence as prosecuting counsel rose and began his opening speech.

'May it please your lordship; members of the jury, in this case I appear on behalf of the prosecution with my learned friend, Mr Dank, and the accused, as you have heard, is not legally represented. The two charges to which he has pleaded not guilty form part and parcel of the same transaction and amount to a particularly wicked and audacious blackmail scheme. It is possible that a number of you may have read something about it in the papers, but, if that is so, I would ask you to put it right out of your minds as it is your duty to try the accused solely on the evidence which is given in this Court and not on anything you may have heard or read about the matter before you came here today.'

Philip Vane had a pleasant, conversational tone which always earned him the attention of a jury who were surprised to find a barrister, dressed up in wig and gown, speaking the same language as themselves. The attentive expression of the jury was matched by that of Herbert himself who sat forward, listening as if to a lecture on a topic of special interest to him.

Counsel continued, 'Before going into the evidence in detail, let me quite briefly outline the facts which have led up to this trial.

'The Shangri-La Bingo Hall in Perkin Street, Putney, holds about three hundred and fifty people and on the night of the sixth of November, which was a Wednesday, it was packed. Late-comers had had to be turned away. At half past eight, the first session got under way and about ten minutes later all hell broke loose when a firework was rolled into the auditorium. It was one of those fireworks that gives off a great deal of coloured smoke and you can imagine, without much description from me, the panic it created. The hall was evacuated midst scenes of considerable confusion and bingo came to an end that evening almost before it had begun. Happily no-one was injured, though the accused can hardly claim any credit for that, and, indeed, the actual amount of damage was wholly disproportionate to the chaos and confusion caused by the introduction of the firework into the auditorium. An area of carpet was scorched and that was about all.

'Bingo being the absorbing game it is, no-one actually saw the firework being placed in the hall, but you will probably have little doubt from the evidence you'll hear that it was pushed through an emergency exit door which opens on to an alleyway running at the side of the hall. However, it is right that I should tell you that no-one was seen doing it, nor is there any direct evidence that the accused was at the scene of the crime.' Out of the corner of his eye, Philip Vane noticed Herbert nod approvingly. Quickly he went on, 'On the other hand, from the events which followed, the prosecution will invite you to say that there is no doubt at all that the person who so recklessly and wickedly introduced that firework into the hall was the accused.'

At this, Herbert made a faint tut-tutting sound which earned him a frown from the judge and a restraining glare from the chief prison officer in the dock with him.

'Those then are the facts which support the charge of criminal damage. But, members of the jury, that was only the beginning. It was by way of being the lever necessary to the blackmail demand which was to follow thirty-six hours later. Thirty-six hours during which no-one knew why the outrage had been perpetrated. And then on the morning of the eighth of November everything became all too clear. I can't do better than read to you now the letter – the typed letter – which was received in the West End office of the managing director of the Shangri-La Bingo Company. It is as follows.' With a faintly theatrical touch, counsel extracted a document from the bundle in front of him and held it up as though it were a royal proclamation.

'"Dear Sir, This letter will end all speculation about last night's incident at your premises in Putney. No, it wasn't the I.R.A. or a prank, but a reminder to you how easy it would be to wreck your business. Just think of all that panic and chaos being repeated once a week, as could so easily happen. Think what effect that would have on Shangri-La's mighty profits. Soon there wouldn't be any as everyone shunned your halls. I'm sure I don't have to go on painting this alarming picture. Anyway, it can all be so simply avoided. All you have to do is to let me know that you're ready to do business. Just put an advert in the *Evening Standard* personal column on 9th November saying, 'Bingo wants to hear more' and I'll let you know my terms. Yours faithfully, Mr. X."

'Then there is a postscript which reads, "If you have any sense you'll tell the police to keep right out of this side of things."

'And then there's a second postscript which reads, "You will note that each 'a' in this letter is typed in red. In my next communication each 'b' will be in red. That is so that you'll know it's genuine and comes from me."'

Philip Vane propped the letter against the ledge in front of him as though returning a piece of valuable porcelain to its shelf. He had read it artfully, imparting nuances damning to Herbert in every sentence. He now paused, aware that he had hooked the jury's interest, and cast a glance in Herbert's direction. Herbert's expression was one of patient reproach, as though he'd never have expected anyone as nice as prosecuting counsel to sink that low. He gave a sad little shake of his head as Vane caught his eye.

Addressing himself to the jury once more, Vane went on, 'Before going further, let us just consider that letter for a few moments. It is saying, is it not, that unless you, the Shangri-La

Bingo Company, do as I say I will ruin your business by creating such panic and chaos that no-one will ever patronise your bingo halls again? In short, I can, and will, bust you. It is a letter which contains all the ingredients of blackmail apart from one, namely an unwarranted demand, though you will have noted that there is the promise of that to come when the writer concludes with the words, "I'll let you know my terms".

'There are two other things to note about that letter. First, it is signed Mr X. Now Mr Xs are not uncommon figures in blackmail cases, but it is usually the cloak of anonymity under which the victim gives evidence. It is rare, if not unprecedented, for the blackmailer to filch that designation.' He paused and peered at the jury over the top of his spectacles. A number of them ventured wispy smiles. 'The other comment I'd like to make about the letter concerns the second postscript. In due course you will see the letter and exact copies of it have been prepared for you, showing each letter "a" typed in red. It was followed later by a second letter in which, as promised, all the "bs" appeared in red.

'That is a detail which has not hitherto been publicly disclosed as revelation of the code might have prejudiced police enquiries.

'Well, of course, the Shangri-La Bingo Company in the shape of its managing director immediately and very properly did inform the police of the receipt of that letter. Despite his postscript, the blackmailer can hardly have expected otherwise seeing that the police were already investigating the incident which preceded the sending of the letter.

'Acting under police instructions, an advertisement was inserted in the personal column of the *Evening Standard* using the words specified and the following day the managing director of Shangri-La received a second letter from Mr X, in which the letter "b" was in every instance typed in red.'

Without taking his eyes off the jury, Vane reached down and picked up another document.

'"Dear Sir, Thought you'd be sensible and I do assure you

that you're doing the right thing. No point in watching your profits take a nose-dive when it can be avoided. And, after all, what is £10,000 to a rich company like yours. Yes, £10,000 is all I'm asking for. It isn't nearly as much as it sounds and, anyway, just think what the alternative would cost. Do that and you'll realise what a reasonable request it is. Now here's what you have to do. Have the money in used £10 notes packed in a brown paper parcel and tied with stout string with a good handle for carrying and leave it in one of the left-luggage lockers at Waterloo Station. Take the key of the locker and hang it on a hook which you'll find beneath seat number 8 in the back row of the Adonis Cinema in Soho. Then go away and forget everything. Bring the police into it or try and set a trap and it'll be your Company and its profits which suffer because then I shall be merciless. If anyone is to be caught, it'll be the Shangri-La Bingo Company. And not just caught, but squashed flat. I give you until the day after tomorrow to accept these terms. Notify your acceptance by placing a message in the personal column of the *Evening Standard* that day saying 'Bingo willing to play ball'. After that, be ready to act at short notice because all you will be given is a time to leave the locker key at the Adonis Cinema. Yours faithfully, Mr X." '

Prosecuting counsel let the document fall from his fingers.

'Well, members of the jury, you may think that was clear enough. There was the unwarranted demand for £10,000 and there were the menaces. Pay me or I'll ruin your business. Add those two ingredients together and you have the offence of blackmail.'

Vane lowered his head and once more peered at the jury over the top of his spectacles.

'The fact that the scheme as devised was impossible of execution,' he went on mildly, 'is neither here nor there, for the offence was already complete.' For a second or two he surveyed with gentle amusement the expectant expressions on the twelve faces on the opposite side of the Court. 'You see, members of the jury, the accused had overlooked one thing, namely that the left-luggage lockers at Waterloo Station have been out of service since we've been having bomb scares. You won't be surprised to hear, however, that no attempt was made to correct the accused's misapprehension and, accordingly, once more acting under police instructions, the Shangri-La Bingo Company inserted the required advertisement in the *Evening Standard* on the day specified.'

While Vane was speaking, a number of jurors glanced towards Herbert to observe his reaction to the disclosure just made. If they expected anything tell-tale or give-away, they were disappointed, for Herbert met their glances with an expression which disclaimed any responsibility for what was being described. 'What an extraordinary story we're being told,' it seemed to say. 'It certainly has nothing to do with me.'

'On that same day as the advertisement appeared,' counsel went on, 'the managing director received a phone call saying that the key was to be left beneath the cinema seat that very evening and not later than half past seven. I may add that the voice making the call was obviously disguised and that the call came from a public box. Police immediately mounted a massive surveillance operation in and around the cinema and a key to one of the disused lockers at Waterloo was placed on a hook which had been thoughtfully provided on the underside of seat number 8 in the back row.

'The programme at the Adonis Cinema is a continuous one, members of the jury, so that there are constant comings and goings in the darkness. That particular evening it consisted of a series of short horror films whose soundtracks were made up almost entirely of hysterical female screams so that the noise in the cinema was considerable.

'Shortly before half past eight the occupant of seat number 8 got up and left. He was followed by police officers and subsequently eliminated from the case. Almost as soon as this person had vacated the seat, the accused moved from a seat in the same row to number 8. He was seen to feel beneath the seat from time to time and after about ten minutes he got up and left. He was followed out of the cinema by officers who had been keeping him under observation. He turned into Shaftesbury Avenue and walked to Piccadilly Circus. There he entered the Underground Station, got a 15p ticket from an automatic machine and descended to the west-bound platform of the Piccadilly Line. He got into the first train and travelled as far as South Kensington. At South Kensington he left the train, went up to the street level and began walking along the Fulham Road. He was about to enter a coffee bar when he was stopped by Detective Sergeant Attwell and Detective Constable Prentice. He agreed to accompany the officers to Canon Row Police Station where he was searched and the key to the disused locker which had been left beneath seat number 8 was found in his right-hand trouser pocket.

'At the police station, he was interviewed by Detective Chief Superintendent Lapham and questioned about his possession of the key. He said he had found it when he was picking up his handkerchief which he had dropped, that he had thought it a funny place for a key to be and that he had best take it and hand it in at the box office on his way out. When asked why he had not done so, he said that he had begun to feel unwell while in the cinema and had consequently left earlier than he'd intended with the one idea in his head of getting out into the fresh air.

'He was also questioned about the firework incident at the Shangri-La Bingo Hall in Putney and about the two letters sent to the company's managing director. He denied all knowledge of these matters.'

'As I still do,' Herbert broke in, vehemently.

'Be quiet,' the judge said. 'You'll have an opportunity of giving the jury your version of events in due course, but you mustn't interrupt prosecuting counsel.'

'I apologise, my lord, but when you're as much the victim of ...'

'Be quiet, I tell you.'

'I'm sorry, my lord, I'll try to restrain myself,' Herbert said, assuming a cowed expression, 'but when you've been held in custody ...'

'I shan't warn you again,' Mr Justice Tidyman interrupted in a grim tone. 'If necessary, your trial will proceed in your absence if you don't behave yourself. I should be extremely reluctant to order such a course, but it's as well that you should know I have the power. Now, try and behave yourself.'

Herbert nodded contritely and appeared to blink away tears which had suddenly come into his eyes, at the same time turning his head in the jury's direction.

'Yes, go on, Mr Vane,' the judge said, deciding to ignore Herbert's blatant attempt to enlist the jury's sympathy. He could only hope that they weren't taken in. In due course he would remind them that they were dealing with facts and not emotion. At least, as judge, he always had the last word in a trial.

For the next hour, prosecuting counsel told the jury the details of the evidence which witnesses would be called to give. Herbert sat listening attentively, making frequent notes and, from time to time, shaking his head sorrowfully. Apart, however, from an occasional 'tsk' he managed to remain silent.

When Vane concluded his opening speech, his junior, Mr Dank, rose to call the first witness.

This was a Mr Lewis who was the manager of the Shangri-La Bingo Hall in Putney. He had a small face, surrounded by a super-abundance of hair which only just stopped short of swamping his features. These were under-pinned by the knot of his tie which was as large as a man's fist and the colour of a harvest moon.

He described how he was standing at the back of the hall observing play when he was suddenly aware of an out-pouring of smoke over on the farther side. He told how he immediately took command of the situation and arranged for an orderly evacuation of the premises. He was at pains to stress that, thanks to Shangri-La's efficient fire drill, no-one was ever in any danger of being injured.

'Do you wish to cross-examine this witness?' Mr Justice Tidyman asked when Mr Dank sat down.

'If you please, my lord,' Herbert said, standing up with a sheaf of notes in one hand.

'Then proceed.'

'Have you ever seen me before, Mr Lewis?' Herbert asked, giving the witness a full frontal stare.

'You're Mr Sipson, aren't you?' Mr Lewis replied in a puzzled tone.

'That's right, but have you ever seen me before?'

'He's never said that he has seen you before,' the judge broke in.

'That's right, I've never said I have,' the witness said, as though suddenly enlightened.

'So you never have seen me before?' Herbert persisted.

'Mr Sipson,' the judge observed with a heavy sigh, 'there's no suggestion on the part of the prosecution that you were observed in the vicinity of this bingo hall on the evening in question. Your question to this witness is accordingly unnecessary.'

'But do the jury understand that, my lord?'

'I'm quite certain they do. Moreover, I shall make it my duty to remind them of the fact when the time comes. Now, do you have any other questions to ask this witness?'

'Yes, my lord.' Turning to Mr Lewis again, Herbert said, 'Do you have any idea at all who threw the firework into the hall?'

'He's already told the jury that he hasn't,' the judge said in an exasperated tone.

'That means he can't say it was me.'

'Mr Sipson, I won't have the jury's time wasted by these unnecessary questions.'

'I'm sorry, my lord. I'm only trying to defend myself.'

'That still doesn't give you licence to ask unnecessary questions.'

Herbert assumed a cowed expression and sat down.

The next witness was a Mrs Ada King beneath whose seat the firework had come to rest. 'Just as I was about to have a full house,' she added, the timing of the incident still obviously rankling.

'What happened then?' Vane asked her.

'What happened?' she echoed scornfully. 'You've never

seen such a bloody shambles in all your life, that's what happened.'

'You were upset?'

'So would you've been, mister.'

'Mrs King, my question wasn't as silly as it sounded. I just wanted to know what your reaction was to the incident.'

'Oh, I was upset all right, though it's not the word I'd have used.'

'It'll probably suffice,' the judge remarked crisply.

A few minutes later, Herbert was asked if he wished to cross-examine the witness.

'Have you ever seen me before?' he asked.

'Never seen you in my life.'

'So you didn't see me on the night in question?'

'Mr Sipson,' the judge said in a grating tone, 'if she's never seen you in her life, it follows she didn't see you that night. Moreover, it has never been suggested by the prosecution that the witness has seen you before.'

'But it's vital to my defence to establish this, my lord.'

'It has already been established *ad nauseam*, Mr Sipson. Do you have any other questions to ask this witness?'

'Not if you are satisfied that I have made my point, my lord.'

'Not only myself, but everyone else in Court must be satisfied as to that by now.' Mr Justice Tidyman glanced up at the clock beneath the public gallery. 'The Court will now adjourn until five minutes past two.'

A few minutes later, the only people left in the court-room were Detective Chief Superintendent Lapham, Detective Sergeant Attwell and the two prosecuting counsel.

'He reminds me of a waiter in a third-rate seaside hotel,' Vane said with a smile. 'I can just see him in an ill-fitting dinner jacket ingratiating himself with the aged residents as he serves them Brown Windsor soup.'

'I can assure you, Mr Vane, there's nothing likeable about the man,' Lapham said severely. 'As far as I'm concerned, he's just a dangerous criminal.'

'He's a singularly unsuccessful one. I've never come across anyone with three previous convictions for blackmail.'

'It's always over-elaborate plans that have been his undoing. It seems he can't resist them. They're his trade-mark. The computer had even coughed up his name before we got on to him.'

'Do you mean to tell me,' Vane asked, 'that my name might be produced by your computer in connection with some crime?'

'Not unless you've a C.R.O. file, sir.'

'Ah! Well, I'm safe for the time being.'

'I reckon the judge is going to be pretty fed-up with him by the end, sir,' Nick Attwell remarked. 'But I expect he reckons that if he gives him enough rope he'll hang himself.'

'An accused who defends himself is a bit like a farmyard hen. Clucking and pecking all over the place and very hard to smother. Incidentally, why has he been so determined to defend himself?'

Lapham shook his head. 'Said at the outset he didn't want a lawyer and has stuck to it.'

'Was he represented at his previous trials?'

'I gather so.'

'Maybe that's the answer then.'

'You don't think there's any chance of his getting off, do you, Mr Vane?'

Philip Vane gave the two officers a bland smile.

'That's the equivalent of asking if the favourite is certain to win the Grand National. You've been around long enough, Mr Lapham, to know that jury trial is as unpredictable as any steeplechase.' Lapham nodded glumly and Vane added, 'And we're not even yet at the first fence.'

It was at this moment that a young Detective Constable entered the court-room and dashed up to where they were talking. Addressing himself to Lapham, he said, 'Will you please phone Deputy Assistant Commissioner Napier right away, sir? It's urgent.'

CHAPTER TWO

Sir Arnold Swallow sat fuming in the back of his Rolls, which was caught in a traffic jam at Shepherd's Bush Green. It was already after ten o'clock and he was normally at his office by a quarter past nine.

But this morning everything had gone wrong. First there had been a power cut when he was in the middle of shaving and this in turn had delayed breakfast. And then when he had emerged from the house expecting to see the car waiting with Mason standing ready to open the rear door for him, there had been no car. A quarter of an hour later when it did arrive, an apologetic Mason explained that he had had to change a wheel because of a puncture.

'A puncture?' Sir Arnold had said in a tone of petulant disbelief as though a Rolls was immune to anything so ordinary.

Thereafter he had settled behind his *Times* and tried to forget the irritating start to the day. Instead of that, however, it was soon apparent that his frustrations were by no means over. The traffic on the motorway was not only heavier at this slightly later hour, but there were a couple of lane closures to aggravate the situation. So with the *Times* read, there was nothing left to do but sit back and silently fume and allocate a mountain of blame among those responsible for what had happened. The Electricity Board, the tyre manufacturers, the Ministry of Transport, each in turn came in for searing condemnation in his mind as he glowered at the hapless Mason's neck.

In the result, the Rolls drew up outside the headquarters of the Swallow Sugar Corporation at about the same moment as Herbert Sipson stepped into the dock at the Old Bailey.

For once, Sir Arnold didn't even wait for Mason to come round and open the door for him. He shot out, across the pavement, past the saluting commissionaire and into the executive lift which whisked him straight to the seventh floor.

His secretary, Miss Gunn, who had been with him over twenty years, greeted his arrival with her customary air of dispassion, though her expression held the merest note of interrogation.

'Everything that could go wrong this morning has done so,' he said as he passed through her office on his way to his own.

'Only Mr Ralph was asking for you,' she replied. 'Shall I let him know that you've now arrived?'

'Just give me a few minutes to look through my mail. Is there much?'

'No. There's only one I've not opened. It's marked "personal and strictly private". I suspect it's from a crank, but I thought I'd better leave it for you, Sir Arnold, in view of its marking.'

'It's not a letter bomb?'

Miss Gunn shook her head. 'No, it's quite thin. Will you tell me when you're ready to see Mr Ralph?'

'Yes.'

Ralph Swallow was his cousin and joint managing director of the company. He was ten years younger than Sir Arnold and together they represented their generation on the board of what was still regarded as a family business, although now a huge public company.

The letter to which Miss Gunn had referred lay to the side of the small, neat pile of those which she had opened. The envelope, which was white and cheap-looking, bore a stamp for first class mail and a London postmark of the previous day. The 'personal and strictly private' which was typed in the top left-hand corner was underlined in red. It was addressed to 'Sir Arnold Swallow, Swallow Sugar Corporation, Swallow House, Baker Street, London, W.1'.

As Miss Gunn had said, the contents were thin, by feel no more than a single folded sheet of paper. It almost certainly was from a crank, in which event it could be quickly dealt with. More quickly than the small pile of opened ones which awaited his attention.

Picking up a small, ivory paper-knife, Sir Arnold slit the top of the envelope and extracted the folded sheet of flimsy paper.

He vaguely noticed that there was no date or address at the top as his eye began to skid over the contents. Suddenly his attention was riveted and he took his eye back to the beginning again.

'Dear Sir,' he read, 'You and your fellow directors must be rubbing your hands at the huge profits made by your Company. I can almost hear the noises of celebration resounding round the directors' famous lunch room which I read about in an article. It must make you proud to think of all the tens of thousands of those familiar yellow bags on all the thousands of supermarket shelves throughout the country. Pretty yellow bags, each with your famous trademark of a swallow in flight and each packed with your famous sugar. But have you ever thought how quickly and easily disaster could strike so that no-one would ever want to touch one of your lovely yellow bags again? Have you? Of course you haven't. But it really could happen. Let me explain. Supposing ground glass was introduced into just a few of those yellow bags which were then placed on the shelves of about a dozen shops in different parts of the country. Supposing ... It's a chilling thought, isn't it? Picture a mother pouring spoonfuls of Swallow sugar over her little boy's breakfast cornflakes. Suddenly the little lad lets out a cry and doubles up in agony. Horrible, wouldn't it be? But I'm sure I've said enough to satisfy you that such a disaster must be avoided at all costs. For disaster it would surely be for your company. Apart from the few unfortunates who suffered genuine injury from swallowing ground glass, there'd be hundreds of others who saw it as an opportunity to sue your company and you might have great difficulty resisting their claims. Everyone would be after your profits, whereas at the moment only one person wants a nibble. A mere £100,000 nibble at that. Namely yours truly. If you wish to learn more put an advert in the personal column of next Tuesday's *Evening Standard* saying, "Swallow has ears" and I'll send you my terms. If you go to the police, I'll know you're not intending to act in good faith and then I shall be forced to show you that I mean business. Nasty but inevitable. Yours truly, Mr X.

P.S. Please note that every "g" in this letter is typed in red. In my next communication it'll be the letter "h". This way, you'll recognise my letters.'

After reading it slowly through a second time, Sir Arnold moved across to the window and stared out. The human mind taking refuge in trivial thoughts at times of crisis, he found himself thinking, 'I might have known something like this was going to happen today.' But, unfortunately, in this instance there was no blame to be handily allocated. Blame, if and when it came, was going to engulf the Swallow Sugar Corporation like an avalanche sweeping over a mountain village.

He crossed back to his desk and used the intercom to tell Miss Gunn to ask Mr Ralph to come and see him immediately.

He's still in a mood, Miss Gunn reflected, as she relayed the message to Ralph Swallow's secretary.

'I'll tell you what I wanted to have a word with you about,' Ralph Swallow said as he entered his cousin's office. Then he caught sight of Sir Arnold's face. 'Is anything wrong?' he asked in a puzzled expression.

'Read this,' the older man said, proffering the letter.

It was two minutes before Ralph looked up and said, 'Do you think it's some kind of a hoax?'

'Do you?'

'No-o.'

'Nor do I.'

'What are we going to do?'

'There are only two courses open to us. Go to the police or not go to the police.'

'And if we don't go to the police straight away, I imagine we try and make contact with this Mr X in the manner described.'

'Or ignore the letter altogether?'

'I don't think we can do that. It'd be too risky.'

'There are risks in every course, assuming the fellow means business. It's just that the risks are different.'

'If we're going to have to bring in the police some time, it's probably best to do so immediately.'

'I think so, too. We'd certainly attract criticism if we didn't seek their help until the affair had got out of hand.'

'Which it could do, if Mr X is serious.'

Sir Arnold shrugged. 'In matters such as these I think we have to recognise that the company's interest and the police interest don't necessarily coincide.'

'But the police interest is the public interest.'

'So it will be said. The point is, Ralph, that bringing in the police will inevitably mean publicity and I can't see any publicity that won't be harmful to our company. If we were able to handle this ourselves, we'd avoid any publicity.'

'The difficulty is we've no idea who we're dealing with,' Ralph Swallow said in a tone full of worry.

'I've been thinking about that. Do we know of anyone who has a particular grudge against us?'

'Against the company? Yes, there is someone as a matter of fact. An ex-employee named Farmer. He worked in the cashier's department here and was given the sack a few months ago.'

'For what reason?'

'There was a suggestion that he'd been fiddling money, but we had no real evidence and couldn't give that as the reason for dismissing him. He was something of a neurotic and nobody cared for him.'

'What's he done to us since he left?'

'Written letters, demanding compensation. Letters which have got nastier and more spiteful as time has passed.'

'Do you think he could have written this?'

'I suppose he could have.'

'If it *is* Farmer, I think we should go to the police now and tell them our suspicions.'

There was a silence and then Ralph Swallow said, 'I think

we shall have to do that, anyway.'

Sir Arnold nodded. 'I think so, too. The risks of not telling the police present a more disagreeable prospect than the consequences of reporting the matter to them.'

'How do you propose we do so?'

'I'll phone the Deputy Commissioner. I've met him a number of times.'

A quarter of an hour later, Sir Arnold and Ralph Swallow were on their way to Scotland Yard in a taxi. Miss Gunn had been sworn to secrecy as to the reason for their journey and its destination. Luckily Mason had taken the Rolls round to a garage to have the puncture repaired so that it was only natural that the commissionaire should be asked to get them a taxi to take them to a meeting in Whitehall. It was not until they were on their way that the driver was told their true destination.

At Scotland Yard they were whisked up to the seventh floor where Deputy Assistant Commissioner Napier of C Department was waiting to see them.

'I gather from the Deputy Commissioner that you've received a blackmail letter of some sort,' the D.A.C. said after introductions had been made and he had explained that the Deputy Commissioner, having made the preliminary arrangements, had had to go to a conference at the Home Office.

'This is it,' Sir Arnold said bleakly, handing him the letter and envelope.

The two men watched him read it with expressions of suppressed expectancy.

'You were certainly right to get in touch with us immediately,' the D.A.C. said as he laid the letter on his desk.

'There was never any question of doing otherwise,' Sir Arnold said quickly. 'I gather you think it's a genuine threat?'

'One can't risk not taking it seriously.'

'It might, I suppose, be a crank,' Ralph Swallow said.

'Cranks can be as dangerous as anyone,' the D.A.C. remarked flatly. 'If the writer of this letter put his threats into effect, there'd be just about the loudest public outcry you've ever heard. It's more diabolical than a plane hijacking or a child kidnapping. We're living in an age of audacious crimes. Soon the Great Train Robbery will seem an old-fashioned affair compared with what's being perpetrated today.'

The two executives of the Swallow Sugar Corporation nodded gravely.

'So what do we do?' Sir Arnold asked.

'We mount a full-scale operation to trap Mr X before he can do any harm. That means that you must insert the required notice in next Tuesday's *Evening Standard* and see what happens. In the meantime, we'll give the letter every scientific check we can think of to find out what we can learn about the paper, the typewriter, the person who licked the stamp. Everything.' He looked from one to the other of the two men facing him. 'It's of the utmost importance to keep the whole operation secret. Is that difficult from your point of view?'

'I'm very glad to hear you say that,' Sir Arnold remarked. 'The last thing the company wants is any publicity.'

'It could, I imagine, be almost as damaging to you as any execution of the threats,' the D.A.C. observed.

'It could indeed,' Sir Arnold replied grimly.

'But the important thing from our point of view is to lure the blackmailer on and do nothing to arouse his suspicions. We mustn't do anything to frighten him off.'

'I think we ought to mention a disgruntled employee who might possibly be responsible,' Ralph Swallow said.

'I was coming to that in a moment. We shall want the names of anyone you suspect. Anyone who has shown a grudge against your company. There are probably quite a few.'

'I don't think so,' Sir Arnold said in an affronted tone. 'We pride ourselves on our excellent relations with the public at large. Equally, we regard ourselves as a model employer. There is this one man my cousin has mentioned, but I assure you that we don't have whole files of dissatisfied customers or employees. Far from it.'

'There are probably more than you think,' the D.A.C.

said, unabashed. 'I'll assign a senior officer to the enquiry and make him personally responsible to me. You'll be at your office the rest of the day?'

Sir Arnold nodded. 'My cousin and I will be at his disposal.'

'Good. I'll tell him to announce himself as plain Mr so as to avoid stirring up gossip when he calls on you. But he'll be a Detective Chief Superintendent.'

'I must say I feel much happier, Mr Napier, now that we've got your assistance in handling this appalling situation.'

'That's what we're here for,' the D.A.C. said cheerfully, rising from his desk. He gazed thoughtfully towards the window for a second or two. 'There is one puzzling aspect of this whole affair I've not mentioned. It bears a number of quite remarkable resemblances to an earlier blackmail attempt.'

'Perhaps it's the same person,' Ralph Swallow said.

'Except that the other person is being tried at this moment and has been in custody for the past two and a half months.'

'Then it obviously can't be the same person,' Sir Arnold observed.

'It would seem not. However, that's our problem to sort out.'

'What's the name of this other man?'

'Herbert Sipson. He tried to take the Shangri-La Bingo Company for a £10,000 ride. You'll probably read about it in the evening paper. The trial only began this morning.'

Sir Arnold turned towards the door. 'Well, if anyone responds to the notice we insert in next Tuesday's *Evening Standard*, it clearly won't be Sipson. Not if he's in custody.'

CHAPTER THREE

D.A.C. Napier arrived at the Old Bailey soon after half past one. He was accompanied by Detective Chief Superintendent Wilcox and they went immediately up to one of the conference rooms on the third floor where the Director of Public Prosecutions and Treasury Counsel have the run of a corridor.

'I'm sorry to cut short your lunch,' the D.A.C. said to Philip Vane, 'but this is something I thought you should know about before you go back into Court this afternoon.'

'I gather there's been a similar demand made on the Swallow Sugar people. Everything obviously hinges on how similar.'

'The approach is almost identical; the demand considerably bigger. Perhaps you'd better take a look at the letter which the chairman of Swallow Sugar received this morning.'

He passed it across the table to Vane, who read it with Lapham and Nick Attwell looking over his shoulder on one side and Dank and the D.P.P.'s representative doing likewise on the other.

'Identical even to using the same recognition code,' Vane said, when he had finished. 'Of such strong similarity as to amount to system in an evidential sense.' He gave the D.A.C. a wry grin. 'So what do we do now, Mr Napier?'

'I know what *we* do. We lay plans to catch the fellow. But what are *you* going to do in the light of this further letter? That seems to me a far less easy question.'

Vane stared out of the window for a second or two.

'Let's take it in stages,' he said in a thoughtful tone. 'Obviously this new development is of great relevance to Sipson's defence. It is information which has come into the possession

24

of the prosecution and which it is their duty to make available to the defence. There can be no question at all about that.' He glanced at Dank who nodded. 'In the ordinary way I'd inform defending counsel and leave him to use the information as he saw fit. But Sipson's not represented and I don't see myself holding an animated colloquy with him over the edge of the dock.' He turned towards Dank again. 'I don't know what you think, Ian, but I think I ought to go and see the judge in his room, tell him what's happened and leave him to impart the information to the accused.'

'I'm sure that's the proper course, Philip,' Dank replied.

'It has the further advantage of drawing the judge's view as to the future conduct of the case,' Vane remarked with a smile.

'Do you think he may suggest that the prosecution should throw in its hand?' the D.A.C. asked.

'I'd doubt it. I think he'll regard it entirely as an issue for the jury. Though having said that, one has to face the fact that it doesn't merely diminish the prospects of a conviction, it virtually extinguishes them. That is, unless your enquiries show conclusively that two different people could have been involved.' He paused. 'And I suppose that's possible,' he added, glancing at the faces round the table.

'I'm certain we haven't got the wrong man in the dock,' Lapham said stoutly. 'Any number of people could have decided to imitate Sipson's attempt to get money out of the Shangri-La Company. Even though the case hasn't had any press publicity to date, quite a few people knew all the details and if each of them told only one person, a whole lot more knew as well. And we can't rule out the possibility that Sipson himself talked. It seems to me, sir,' he went on energetically, 'to be jumping to conclusions to say that one person must be behind both crimes.'

'Everything is going to depend on timing,' Vane broke in. 'In other words, are you going to be able to produce evidence which will shatter Sipson's now greatly strengthened defence before the end of his trial is reached?'

The D.A.C. pursed his lips. 'It looks as if we must pursue two lines of enquiry at the same time. One to catch the man who is threatening Swallow Sugar, the other to ascertain what Sipson may have got up to while he's been in custody. We'll need to find out who his visitors have been and who he has been writing to.' He turned to Detective Chief Superintendent Lapham. 'I think it's very important, Fred, that you and Jack maintain a firm liaison and I should like to detach Sergeant Attwell from the present case for that purpose. Can you manage without his constant attendance during the trial?'

'He's a witness, sir.'

'Oh, I'm not proposing to spirit him away completely, but I'd like to feel he wasn't tied to the Old Bailey, but is available to advise Jack on the details of the Sipson case as required. He'd certainly have to keep in touch with you and put in an appearance here at least once a day. That would be part of the plan.'

The two senior officers nodded their agreement, leaving Nick to reflect ruefully that his baby could be walking before he even saw it. One consolation was that he had considerable respect and liking for Detective Chief Superintendent Wilcox who was a more sympathetic character than Lapham.

Philip Vane rose. 'I must get back to Court. I'll go and see the judge at the end of the day. It's too late now and, anyway, it's not going to affect the course of events this afternoon.'

They filed out of the conference room, counsel, Lapham and Nick Attwell to return to Court, the D.A.C. to drive back to the Yard and Wilcox to visit Swallow House to start his enquiries and lay plans to entrap Mr X.

As soon as the judge had taken his seat, Vane said, 'I am wondering, my lord, if you'd think I could dispense with the next two witnesses. They are, of course, here and I am happy to tender them for cross-examination, but their evidence relates solely to what happened in the Perkin Street bingo hall when the firework was thrown in and there doesn't seem to be any dispute between the prosecution and defence as to that aspect of the case. In those circumstances, I don't wish to waste the Court's time in calling unnecessary witnesses.'

Mr Justice Tidyman nodded and looked across at Herbert whose expression immediately became one of respectful attention.

'I don't know if you followed that, Mr Sipson?' the judge said. 'As your defence is that you weren't near this bingo hall when the firework was introduced and as you haven't disputed the effect of its introduction, I take it that you don't wish the prosecution to call further evidence relating to that aspect. You've had copies of the statements made by the two witnesses in question served on you, have you not?'

Herbert bowed. 'I am in your lordship's hands,' he said in his most ingratiating tone.

'This is a matter for you,' the judge replied tartly. 'Do you wish to cross-examine these two witnesses bearing in mind that their evidence does nothing to implicate you in that part of the case?'

'If your lordship is satisfied that justice will be done without their evidence, I have nothing further to say,' Herbert said, giving the jury a helpless shrug.

Mr Justice Tidyman bit the tip of his thumb in a determined effort to restrain himself from making any of the acerbic observations that jostled in his mind for utterance.

'I agree, Mr Vane, that it will not assist the jury to hear the next two witnesses and will only waste the time of the Court.' He turned towards the jury and explained the position to them with the patient and kindly air of a protector and friend. Let Sipson realise that he didn't have the sole prerogative of playing up to the jury!

The next witness to be called was the manager of the Adonis Cinema. He was a short, swarthy man of the name of Bernard Kalis. His evidence was brief and consisted of describing the lay-out of the cinema and of stating that the hook found under seat 8 in the back row had not been placed there by the management or to its knowledge.

'Do you have any questions you wish to ask this witness?'

the judge asked Herbert in a resigned tone when Mr Kalis'
examination-in-chief had been concluded.

Herbert nodded keenly and turned in the witness's direction.

'Were you at the cinema on the night I was arrested?'

'Yes.'

'Did you see me?'

'I think I may have done.'

'But you're not sure?'

'Mr Sipson,' the judge broke in, his tone one of heavily
strained patience, 'are you saying that you were not in the
Adonis Cinema that evening?'

'No, my lord, I was. I thought that was clear.'

'So did I. And if you were there, does it matter whether
this witness is sure or not sure that he saw you?'

'If your lordship pleases,' Herbert said with a further small
bow.

'Do you think you may have seen me?'

'I may have done.'

'And if you did see me, did you see me carrying any
screws?'

'Screws?' the judge exclaimed. 'What on earth are you
talking about?'

'The prosecution suggest I put a screw underneath the
seat where the key was.'

'So?'

'I didn't.'

'If this witness is uncertain whether or not he may have
seen you that evening, it is quite pointless asking him if he
saw you carrying a screw into the cinema. Apart from anything else, he has never said so.'

'I am obliged to your lordship for making the point so
clearly.'

'Have you any more questions to ask this witness?' the
judge asked in a tone of dread.

'Did you see me leave the cinema?'

'Yes.'

'You did?'

'Yes.'

'Where were you?'

'In the foyer.'

'Why did you see me leave?'

'Because I was standing there.'

'Who else was standing in the foyer?'

'There were a number of policemen in plain clothes.'

'Were they pretending to be patrons?'

'I think that was the general idea.'

'How did I look?'

'I don't follow you.'

'Did I look sick?'

'I'd say worried more than sick.'

'Anxious perhaps?'

'If you like.'

'Anxious to get out into the fresh air because I was feeling ill?'

Mr Justice Tidyman dropped his pen and uttered a strangled sound. 'That is not a question the witness can possibly answer. Indeed, it is not a question at all, it's a piece of evidence.'

'I have only one more question, my lord,' Herbert said in a meek tone.

The judge nodded curtly and stretched to retrieve his pen which had rolled across the desk.

'Do you agree, remembering how ill I looked, that it was reasonable I forgot to hand in the key I'd found beneath my seat?'

'Don't attempt to answer that question,' the judge interjected. 'Is that all?' he asked, staring implacably at Herbert.

'Do I gather, my lord, that you disallow my question?'

'You do.'

Herbert gave a small perplexed shrug and glanced quickly at the jury before resuming his seat.

The remainder of the afternoon passed without ruction, with Herbert seemingly slumped in a state of increasing dejection. From being an ingratiating-looking-waiter he had in Philip Vane's eyes turned into one on whom it had slowly dawned that his expectations of a good tip were not going to be fulfilled.

At a quarter past four when the Court adjourned, Vane sent a message via the judge's clerk asking if he might see the judge. A few minutes later he found himself in Mr Justice Tidyman's room, where the judge was in the process of removing his robes.

'Hope I'm not giving the jury any impression of bias,' he said over his shoulder as Vane came in, 'but I find that fellow Sipson so repellent it's difficult not to show one's feeling at times.'

Vane smiled. 'I agree, judge, he's an unattractive little man. He also knows how to play up to the jury.'

'He's had enough practice,' Mr Justice Tidyman grunted. 'All that injured innocence, it's enough to make anyone's gorge rise.' He sighed. 'I just hope the jury are not taken in. I'd like to see their faces if they were told he'd been in prison three times already for blackmail. And why do you imagine he's so intent on defending himself? Don't answer that because you might tell me something I'd better not know, but I'm absolutely certain he's going to get up to something in the course of the trial, if only to try to provoke me into perpetrating a miscarriage of justice.' He finished putting on his tie and turned away from the mirror to which he had been addressing his remarks. 'Anyway, Philip, you want to see me about something, what is it?'

'I was given this during the lunch adjournment,' Vane said, handing the judge a copy of the letter which had been sent to the Swallow Sugar Company.

As soon as the judge had read it and before he could make any comment, counsel went on to explain the circumstances of its receipt.

'It's clearly the prosecution's duty to make it available to the defence and it occurred to me, judge, that, as Sipson is not represented, this should be done through you.'

'I'd have to do it in the absence of the jury,' the judge observed in a meditative tone.

Vane gave a quick nod. 'There is a further point I ought to mention. The police are most anxious that there shouldn't be any publicity of this demand on Swallow Sugar. One can see how it could complicate, if not harm, their enquiries if the whole thing got into the newspapers when they're hoping to trap the writer of the letter.'

Mr Justice Tidyman looked thoughtful. 'Yes I can see that,' he said slowly. 'Particularly as the letter tells Swallow not to go to the police and says explicitly that the author of it will carry out his threat if they do.' He paused. 'We're in a dilemma, aren't we? One can't impart the information to Sipson and at the same time tell him not to use it in his defence, because that's the whole reason for giving it to him. On the other hand I can't put a ban on the press from reporting it if and when it comes out in the course of the trial. So what do I do?'

'Of course the press will still be in Court when you give Sipson the information, even though you've sent the jury to their room.'

'I see no problem in asking them not to report what happens at that stage. Indeed it's normal practice for them to observe reticence in respect of anything that passes in the course of a trial in the absence of the jury. No, it's when Sipson uses the information in his defence that the difficulty arises. It's really a matter of timing.' He glanced again at the copy of the letter. 'Today's Thursday, so we have two full days to go, Friday and Monday, before this advertisement appears in the *Evening Standard* next Tuesday.'

'It's really three days, judge, as the police won't be in a position to set their trap until after it has appeared, which means Wednesday at the earliest.'

'Hmm. Well, I can slow down the trial. I might even consider making an excuse not to sit on Monday. Moreover, is there any reason why I have to let the accused have this information immediately? Supposing I wait until the end of tomorrow, rather than do it first thing when the Court sits? After all, as long as he knows before he opens his defence, it's not prejudicing him. It's not matter for cross-examination of your witnesses still to come; though I have no doubt that Mr Sipson would regard it as such.'

'I suppose he might wish to use it when the police give evidence.'

'Well, that won't be until late tomorrow at the earliest at our present rate of progress.'

'We've been talking, judge, in the terms of Sipson's trial continuing,' Vane said, after a pause, 'I take it that is your considered view?'

Mr Justice Tidyman looked up sharply. 'Most certainly. It's for the jury to decide what they make of this development. You weren't proposing to throw in your hand, were you?'

'Not unless you gave my arm a judicial twist,' Vane said with a slight grin.

'I have no intention of doing so. I may have to temper some of my observations to the jury when I come to sum up, but I shall still hope they convict him of a wicked and unscrupulous attempt at extortion.'

'Then you don't think we've got an innocent man in the dock.'

'No, I don't,' the judge said emphatically. 'Whatever the explanation, I'm certain it doesn't involve Sipson's innocence.'

'I doubt whether the jury will feel the same for all that.'

The judge pulled a face. 'I concede that I wouldn't wish to place a bet on the jury's verdict. However, much may have happened before we reach that stage.'

'I'm not sure what I think,' Vane observed in a bemused tone. 'I felt we had a reasonably strong circumstantial case against Sipson, but this letter to Swallow Sugar suggests such a remarkably similar *modus operandi* to the one sent to Shangri-La Bingo that I find it very difficult to believe they weren't sent by the same person. And if they were, then it can't have been Sipson.'

'There are a lot of ifs and buts in that assumption,' the judge remarked. 'One day the explanation will emerge and I'll bet you a dollar it won't involve Sipson's innocence. If I really believed him to be innocent, I might put pressure on you to abandon the prosecution. As it is, let the jury bring their proverbial good sense to bear on the issues.' His eyes glinted behind his spectacles as he added, 'Though unhappily not as proverbial as it used to be once. Indeed, I sometimes wonder if we've not hypnotised ourselves over the alleged virtues of jury trial.' He smiled thinly. 'Only *sometimes*, mark you.'

While Philip Vane had been seeing the judge, Nick Attwell had been on his way to Brixton Prison, his path ahead smoothed by a phone call from D.A.C. Napier to the Governor himself.

When he arrived, he was escorted to an office in the administrative block where Chief Prison Officer Gillam was waiting for him.

'I gather from the Governor that you're interested in Sipson and I've been told to answer any questions as well as I can,' Gillam said, after the two men had shaken hands.

'We're particularly interested to know who his visitors have been while he's been in custody. Also details of his letter-writing if you have them.'

Gillam nodded. 'I've made enquiries about both those matters, as the Governor gave me an idea what you'd be wanting to know. As to visitors, he hasn't had any. Not one. So that's easily answered. As to his letters, I've had a word with the officers who saw most of him and it seems he never received any. So no visitors and no letters.'

'Presumably he didn't write any either?'

'Certainly no record of his having written any.' Gillam gave a rueful shrug. 'Though it's not exactly unknown for a prisoner to get a letter smuggled out. A remand prison's a bit like a transit camp with all the arrivals and departures.'

'From what you say, he doesn't appear to have either family or friends.'

'Not of the visiting variety, anyway. One of the prison officers to whom I spoke told me that he made some comment to Sipson about his absence of visitors and Sipson was a bit indignant – I suppose he thought he was being slurred – and said he had a sister-in-law who would be very glad to visit him, but she lived too far away.'

Nick gave a weary sigh.

'Anything else you can tell me about him while he's been here?'

'He hasn't given any trouble, if that's what you mean.'

'Has he been popular with the staff?'

Gillam shook his head. 'He's been neither popular nor unpopular. He's done as he's been told, and kept himself to himself.'

'He hasn't been particularly pally with any fellow prisoner?'

Gillam again shook his head, this time with an air of helplessness. 'If Sipson had been a trouble-maker, we might have noticed him rather more. But I'm afraid he's passed unnoticed amongst Brixton's population. We can start observing him a bit more closely now if that's any use?'

'I doubt whether it will be.'

Ten minutes later, Nick was driving himself back to the Yard against the tidal flow of homeward-bound commuter traffic.

Not for the first time he pondered over the changes which had taken place in his life during the past twelve months. The major ones, of course, had been marriage to Woman Detective Constable Clare Reynolds, and not long after that event, his transfer from division to C.1. at the Yard.

He had viewed the transfer with mixed feelings. From outside its ranks, the Yard gave the appearance of a large, soulless headquarters where the hours might be more regular but the fun of working would be considerably less. As things turned out, he was wrong on both counts. His hours of work were as unpredictable as they had been on division and he didn't experience the stifling of his independence that he had feared. Nevertheless, he did miss the camaraderie of a small divisional C.I.D., though this could be shattered by a difficult guvnor, not that Nick had any substantial grumbles against the two under whom he had served in his particular division.

Anyway, if you wanted to get on, you went where you were

told and did what was asked of you as effectively as possible. And Nick did want to get on. Not only because he enjoyed being a police officer, in particular being a detective, but because he now had a wife to look after and there'd soon be a baby, too.

When he reached the room which he shared with three other Detective Sergeants, he found a message on his desk asking him to go and see Detective Chief Superintendent Wilcox immediately on his return.

Nick had always thought that Wilcox looked more like an actor playing the part than the real thing. He was a good-looking man in his early forties, with grey eyes and thick iron grey hair. He was always well-dressed, but not obtrusively so, and he was apt to make theatrical play with a pair of heavy black-rimmed spectacles. It was this, more than anything else, that put Nick in mind of his being an actor.

As Nick entered his room, Wilcox was staring across at the far wall swinging his spectacles in front of him in a nonchalant fashion.

'Good, you're back,' he said, putting them on with a flourish and then almost immediately taking them off again. 'What did you find out at Brixton?'

Nick told him.

'That doesn't take us much farther,' he remarked. 'Indeed, I'm not sure there's much mileage to be got out of any enquiries until after Swallow Sugar insert their advert in next Tuesday's *Standard*. However, I suppose we must go through the motions of doing something and I thought we might pay a visit this evening to Heston.'

'Heston? Isn't that somewhere near Heathrow Airport, sir?'

'That's right. It's also the last known address of one Jeffrey Farmer, dismissed employee of Swallow Sugar.'

'They think he may be behind this?'

'His is the only name they've come up with as a possibility. He was sacked three months ago for a suspected cash fiddle. They didn't have much evidence, but they decided to get rid of him, anyway. He seems to have been one of those prickly people who was always getting on the wrong side of everyone and they were glad to have the opportunity of being shot of his services. However, it doesn't seem that he went at all willingly and though they did finally give him the push, he reacted with considerable bitterness and has since shown a fair amount of vindictiveness.'

'In what way, sir?'

'First of all, he paraded up and down the pavement outside Swallow House with a placard saying, "Swallow sugar is sweet, Swallow's directors are sour bastards". The police were eventually called and he was warned that he'd be arrested and charged with conduct likely to cause a breach of the peace if he didn't pack it in. The company wasn't keen on court proceedings and luckily he accepted the warning and decamped. Thereafter, however, he has sent the managing director a number of abusive letters, the last of which was only received a week ago and gloated at the fact that the company's shares had taken a dive on the stock market.'

'I take it, they didn't reply to any of his letters?'

'No, they didn't.'

'So he may well have been considering ways of hotting up his campaign to make them take notice.'

Wilcox nodded. 'Exactly. He sounds an unstable fellow and ... well, putting ground glass into bags of sugar could be the sort of thing his obviously twisted mind could think up. So I thought we'd go and have a scout around where he lives and see if we can find out anything useful. We'll need to be careful as we don't want to scare him off if he *is* the villain in our piece, until we're sure he's put the rope round his neck. We'll have to play it by ear.'

'I take it, sir, we don't disclose that we're police officers?'

'We'll think of a suitable cover while we're driving there. Are you ready to go now?'

'May I just make a quick phone call to my wife?'

'Sure. Expecting a baby, isn't she?'

Nick grinned. 'In about a month.'

'Right, I'll wait for you here.' Wilcox picked up his spectacles off his desk and slipped them into his breast pocket with the flourish of a conjuror.

They went in Nick's car and it was while they were on the way that Wilcox said suddenly, 'We'll say we've come on some insurance matter. Insurance men often call after office hours, it's the only time they can find people at home.'

In Nick's experience, insurance men worked the same hours as most other people and, if they did make an evening call, it was usually by appointment. It was as though Wilcox read his thoughts for he added in an offhand tone, 'We needn't work out anything very elaborate.'

When they arrived in the area, Nick went into a pub to enquire the way to Clearview Road which turned out to be about three-quarters of a mile away.

Parking the car at the end of the road, they walked up until they came to number 28, which like all the other houses was a semi-detached with a Snowcem façade. A short path led from the front gate to the porch of the house.

The wood of the gate had swollen and Wilcox had to wrestle with it before he managed to open it.

'It's almost as bad as my own at home,' he remarked as he gave himself a quick brush-down following his contest with the obstacle.

The house appeared to be in darkness, but soon after Wilcox had pushed the bell, a light came on in the hall. There was the sound of a key being turned and the door was opened to the extent of the chain which they had heard being put in position.

A woman's frowning face peered at them.

'Would you be Mrs Farmer?' Wilcox asked in a quietly polite tone.

'Mrs Farmer, did you say?' The woman's tone was a mixture of suspicion and hostility. 'Who told you I was Mrs Farmer?'

'No-one did. I guessed you might be. Obviously wrong. I'm sorry.'

'I'm Miss Burnett. I had a lodger called Farmer once. A Mr Jeffrey Farmer.'

'A-Ah. That's obviously where the confusion has arisen, Miss Burnett. But did you say *once*?'

'He left about a month ago.'

'Can you tell me his present address? We're from his insurance company. He ought to have notified us of his change of address, but it's obviously slipped his mind to do so.'

'I don't know where he's staying, but I believe he's still in the district. Mr Illingham was telling me a few days ago that he'd seen him in *The Three Ducks*.'

'Is that the pub back on the corner of the main road?' Nick asked. 'I went in there to enquire the way to Clearview Road but never noticed the name.'

'No, that's the *Rising Sun*. *The Three Ducks* is in the other direction.'

Wilcox took a step nearer the door and said in a confidential voice, 'It occurs to me, Miss Burnett, that you may be able to help us quite considerably if you can spare a few minutes.' As she slipped the chain off the door, he added with a deprecating smile, 'I hope we're not taking you away from a favourite T.V. programme.'

'It doesn't start for another half hour,' she replied.

'Oh, that's fine. We'll be out of your way by then.'

She led them to her back parlour in which three of the five chairs were occupied by sleeping cats. She gestured Wilcox and Nick to the two free ones, which also happened to be the two hardest, and plucked a large marmalade cat off the most comfortable-looking one, settling it on her lap as she sat down.

'As you probably realise, Miss Burnett,' Wilcox said smoothly, 'much of our time is taken up in confidential enquiries concerning our clients and the company has recently been a little worried about Mr Farmer. He's been difficult to contact and oh ... well, I don't have to trouble you with all the details, but it may be you can throw some light on his recent conduct.'

It became apparent from Miss Burnett's expression as Wilcox was talking that she was not only bursting to throw light on her ex-lodger's behaviour, but also had a quite obvious dislike of him.

'He was only with me two months. He came shortly before he left Swallow Sugar and he went a month later. Something told me he wasn't the right type for my house, but I felt sorry for him as he told me he had nowhere to go and had had to leave his previous place when they wanted his room for their daughter who'd just got divorced.'

Wilcox nodded encouragingly. He was a good listener and listening formed a large part of a detective's work. You never knew when you weren't going to learn something of interest midst all the verbal dross.

'Did he tell you why he left Swallow Sugar?'

'He just said they'd treated him very unfairly. In fact, he kept on about it if you gave him the chance. He was all knotted up inside if you understand what I mean.'

'Didn't think too kindly of his ex-employer, eh?' Wilcox said jovially.

'He was filled with real hate, he was.'

'Did he get another job before he left here?'

'No. That was the trouble. He just spent every day brooding over what had happened. It wasn't healthy.'

'And in the end you asked him to leave?'

'I had it in mind when he upped and went on his own.'

'Did he owe you any money?'

'Not likely. I saw to that.'

'And he never left you any forwarding address?'

'No. He called round once to see if there were any letters for him, which there weren't. I wasn't in, but my friend was here and told me he'd been.'

'But you understand he's been seen in *The Three Ducks*?'

'That's what Mr Illingham told me. He was friendly with Mrs Dove. Mr Farmer, that is.'

'Mrs Dove?'

'She runs *The Three Ducks*.'

Wilcox got up. 'You've really been very helpful, Miss Burnett and my company will be most grateful. I can assure you that everything you've told us will be treated with the utmost confidence and I would ask that you regard our visit in the same light. That is, keep it to yourself, eh!'

He gave Miss Burnett's shoulder a knowing and friendly pat, as though they were mutual confidants of long standing.

Miss Burnett flushed with pleasure and Nick reflected that it was probably many years since she had received anything as compromising from a good-looking man.

Before she could unburden herself of the marmalade cat which pinned her to the chair, Wilcox had moved to the door. 'Don't disturb your cat. We can see ourselves out, Miss Burnett. Thank you again for your help.'

As they walked back to their car, Nick said, 'You had her eating out of your hand, sir.'

'If we'd stayed any longer, she'd have given us each a saucer of milk,' Wilcox said with a laugh. 'Instead of which let's go and sample the beer at *The Three Ducks*.'

Like many public houses, it was strategically placed on a corner. In one direction ran a residential road and in the other there were a number of small shops on either side and then the road narrowed and there were houses. The whole district, including *The Three Ducks*, had grown up in the thirties and owed its haphazard appearance to that era.

The public bar entrance was in one road and that to the saloon bar round the corner in the other.

'My guess is that he's a saloon bar man,' Wilcox said as they gave the outside of the premises a quick survey before entering.

There were fewer than a dozen people in the saloon bar and Nick reckoned most of them were regulars. You could usually tell. The regulars gave the appearance of belonging. There was the lone drinker hunched over the counter at one end, staring morosely at what was probably his fifth or sixth pint. There were two women and a man at a table, who looked as though they'd been there since opening time and wouldn't leave until last orders had been called. The man was an obvious wag and the two women were his loud and appreciative audience.

There were also a number of men putting off the moment of going home. They were the ones who called in each evening on their way back from work and who, for one reason or another, spun out their visits as long as they reasonably could – and probably beyond.

Nick had noticed the licensee's name, Minnie Dove, above the outside of the door and wondered whether the woman they saw standing behind the bar was her. She was at one end by the cash register watching the young barman drawing a pint of beer.

She was short and, without being actually plump, had what might be described as a comfortable figure. She had platinum blonde hair which was heavily lacquered and crowned by an obviously false bun of slightly different colour.

She glanced towards the two officers as they came towards the bar.

'Good evening, gentlemen,' she said pleasantly and smiled. It was a much nicer smile than Nick would have expected. Warm and natural and not just a baring of teeth.

'Two pints of bitter, please,' Wilcox said.

She moved away and drew the beer herself.

'Nice place you have here,' Wilcox observed, when she returned.

'You've not been in before, have you?' she countered.

'No, we don't live in the district. Just passing through.'

'Didn't think I'd seen you.'

Wilcox put his glass down and licked his lips. 'Nice beer, too. What about something for yourself?'

'Thanks. I'll have a small whisky.'

After she had fetched herself the drink, they raised their glasses to one another.

'Cheers,' said Wilcox.

'Cheers,' said Nick.

The woman said nothing, but gave a small nod, watching them closely all the while.

'I imagine you mostly have regulars?' Wilcox remarked idly, glancing around the bar.

41

'And which of them is it you're interested in?'

Wilcox swung round sharply. 'Why do you say that?'

The woman shrugged as though neither question nor answer mattered very much to her.

'I could tell as soon as you came in. We don't get many casuals here and you had a look about you which said you'd come in for a purpose. Information is what people usually come into pubs for, apart from drinking.'

Wilcox smiled. 'That's pretty smart of you, Mrs ...'

'Dove. I'm the licensee.'

'I'd guessed as much. Actually, we're from Green Star Insurance. We've been making a few discreet enquiries about one of our clients and we understand he comes in here from time to time.'

Mrs Dove took a sip of her drink and then turning her back on those nearest to them, she said in a low tone, 'Who's the client?'

'Someone called Farmer,' Wilcox said quietly. 'Is he in here?'

Mrs Dove shook her head. 'He'd be in by now if he was coming.'

'When did you last see him?'

'Two evenings ago.'

'No chance of his coming in this evening?'

'Not now.'

'Do you happen to know his address?'

'No. He's always shifting around anyway.'

'But he lives in the locality?'

'Oh, yes.'

While they had been talking, they had all edged their way slowly to the end of the bar up against the wall where it was possible to speak normally without danger of being overheard.

'It's all in connection with his life policy,' Wilcox remarked in a confidential manner; as though this would satisfactorily explain everything Mrs Dove might be wondering.

'What exactly do you want to know about him?' she

enquired in a tone in which Nick thought he detected a small note of suspicion.

'How has he struck you recently?'

Mrs Dove put a red finger-nail up to the corner of her mouth and delicately removed an imaginary crumb while she stared with a heavy frown into her half-finished drink.

'To be absolutely frank, I've been a bit worried about him. I don't know if you know he lost his job about a month ago. Since that happened, he doesn't seem to have been himself. It's sort of taken over his mind if you understand.'

'You mean, he'd become obsessed about it?'

'Yes, that's it. He could talk of nothing else. Some of my regulars had begun to avoid his company, but I felt sorry for him. And, anyway, it's part of my job to listen to their troubles.'

'I'm sure you do it very sympathetically, too,' Wilcox remarked.

'I try and help if I can,' she said, throwing a sudden look at Nick as though he might be going to contradict her. He quickly gave her an understanding nod.

'Our records show that he used to work for Swallow Sugar,' Wilcox said, 'did you ever hear him speak of that company?'

'That's what I'm saying. He was always on about them after he got the sack.'

'Bitter, you mean?'

'Swearing he'd have his revenge.'

'That's very interesting,' Wilcox said. 'Did he ever say what sort of revenge he had in mind?'

'No, he didn't ever get as far as that.'

'Do you think he really meant it?'

'I wouldn't like to say. You never know, do you, when people get that upset? Difficult to tell how much is just talk. Generally, the more they talk, the less they act.'

'That's true. But it's not always the case.'

There was a silence. Then Mrs Dove said, 'Want me to give him a message when he next comes in?'

Wilcox shook his head quickly. 'No, we'll try and trace him, so don't trouble.'

'No trouble. I can easily tell him you were looking for him about his insurance. If you leave me a number, he can ring you.'

Nick gave Wilcox a faintly anxious look, but his Detective Chief Superintendent appeared unperturbed by the turn of the conversation.

'Actually the whole matter is a bit confidential, Mrs Dove, and it would be better if he didn't know we'd been enquiring about him. Some policy-holders can get quite nasty if they think we've been trying to find out things behind their backs. They don't seem to realise the company has to make enquiries.' He smiled expansively. 'If we didn't do that, we'd soon be out of business.'

'I won't tell him anything then,' Mrs Dove said.

'Do you think he may come in tomorrow?'

'I just can't tell you. He's not one of those who comes in regular-like at the same hour on a certain evening. All one can say of him is that if he's not in by half past seven, he won't be in at all.'

'Well, it's been nice talking to you, Mrs Dove, but it's time my colleague and I were on our way. If we're ever in the district again, we'll know where to come for a pint.' He stretched across the bar to shake hands and Nick followed suit.

As they made their way to the door, Nick noticed the same people who'd been there when they arrived. Either it wasn't a very busy evening, or it simply wasn't a busy pub. He noticed a sign near the door advertising the 'attraction' of a pianist every Saturday evening. Perhaps that brought in a few more customers, though it certainly wouldn't draw him.

'We'll drop by the local station before we go back,' Wilcox said when they were in the car.

It was about a mile away and a sergeant was passing through the otherwise deserted enquiry office as they entered.

'Can I help you?' he asked with a marked absence of enthusiasm.

Wilcox introduced himself and Nick and the sergeant said

defensively, 'I'm afraid this place is like a pub after closing time.'

'Do you have anything on a man named Farmer who lives in the district?' Wilcox asked, ignoring the other's comment.

'Never heard of him, sir. What's his address?'

'That's the difficulty, I don't know it. He seems to change his lodgings quite frequently. He was last with a Miss Burnett in Clearview Road.'

'Like us to try and run him to earth, sir?'

'I'd like you to put out a few discreet feelers and let me know if you find out where he's staying.'

'You don't want him picked up?'

'Definitely not. Just tell your lads to keep their eyes and ears open as to his present whereabouts.'

'I'll do that, sir.'

Wilcox seemed about to turn away, but suddenly asked, 'Why isn't *The Three Ducks* better patronised?'

'Never has been. It's a poor location for a pub. Not enough regulars and off the beaten track for casuals. Minnie Dove does her best, but it's not enough.'

'What's her reputation?'

'Minnie?' The sergeant gave a short laugh. 'She's had as many men in her life as I've had hot dinners.'

'Is there a Mr Dove?'

'I think he was her second or third husband. But that was several years ago. She's given up marrying them now.'

Wilcox smiled. 'Thanks for your help.'

It was shortly before half past nine when Nick arrived home at the small house just off Barnes Common which he and Clare had acquired on marriage.

Clare was sitting on a hard chair at the kitchen table with an evening paper spread out in front of her.

She heard the key turn in the front door, but scarcely had time to look round before Nick had bounded into the kitchen. She tilted her head to receive his kiss.

A second later he stood back and gave her a worried look as he placed his hand on her forehead.

'You feel hot, darling,' he said, anxiously.

Clare sighed. 'I feel hot because I am hot, and I am hot because I've been standing at the stove.' She smiled at him fondly. 'I never really believed that the modern expectant father still behaved like one of Dickens's more sentimental characters.' She squeezed his hand. 'But I'd sooner you were that way than that you used my condition as an excuse to chat up a barmaid.'

'As a matter of fact, that's precisely what I've been doing, chatting up a barmaid. Want to hear about it?'

'Let me get your supper out of the oven and then I'm all ears.'

'Aren't you eating too?'

'I had something earlier. I'll just make myself another cup of coffee. Are you ready now?'

'Ready!' he cried out, miming the firing of a starting pistol.

It was while her back was turned, taking dishes from the oven that she heard him go out of the kitchen and dash upstairs to the bathroom. Putting food on the table at meal-times had always been the signal for him to depart from the room. At first, she had tried to cajole him into going to do whatever he wanted to do before she actually dished up. 'Yes, darling, I'm ready now,' he'd say and remain where he was until she had put the food on the table, when he would make his dash upstairs. She had even discussed the vexing habit with a worldly neighbour who had remarked, 'All men are the same. It's a hang-over from when they were little boys and regarded peeing and washing hands as an exasperating intrusion into playtime. You'll never cure him.'

She heard the toilet flush and half a minute later he was back in the kitchen.

'That does smell good,' he said eagerly as he sat down in front of a plate of steak and kidney pie and brussels sprouts. 'Are you sure Master Attwell wouldn't like some?'

'Quite sure.'

'How's he been today?'

'Clumping around in army boots by the feel of him this afternoon.'

Nick was so certain that the baby would be a boy that he always referred to him as Master Attwell. Clare was neither so certain, nor for that matter so caring, but went along with his fancy. She knew that if it turned out to be Miss Attwell he would be just as pleased.

'Tell me about this barmaid you've been chatting up,' she said, as she joined him at the table with her mug of coffee.

For the next twenty minutes, she listened intently while Nick related the day's events.

'What do you make of it?' he asked at the end.

'It seems as if someone must have learnt of Herbert Sipson's scheme to blackmail the Shangri-La Bingo Company and decided to improve on it to extort money from Swallow Sugar. After all, the two schemes may have basic similarities, but this later one is a far smoother operation. I mean the threat of throwing fireworks into bingo halls is nothing like as sophisticated as the threat of introducing ground glass into packets of Swallow Sugar. The one is clumsy and full of risks whereas the other is as foolproof and undetectable as you can get. There'd be national panic if so much as a rumour reached the public.'

'I know. It's a grim thought that whoever it is probably has bags of contaminated sugar all ready to put on supermarket shelves. That's why we have to trace Farmer without delay. If it is him, the whole diabolical plot can be nipped in the bud. And if it isn't, well, at least we'll have eliminated him from the enquiry.'

'Was he the only person Swallow Sugar could suggest as a possible suspect?'

'Apparently.'

'A hundred thousand pounds is an awful lot of money,' Clare said in a thoughtful tone.

'From all accounts, Farmer was an extremely bitter man. He might easily have made it half a million or even a million.'

'Those sort of sums would be more in keeping with someone who's lost touch with reality.'

'I'm not sure I follow you.'

'Well, a hundred thousand is a practical sum. The company can afford it and one can even envisage their paying it to avoid a catastrophe. But not half a million.' She paused. 'What I'm trying to say is that someone who is motivated entirely by spite and vengeance might demand half a million. The bigger the sum, the greater balm for his injured feelings. But someone who asks only for a hundred thousand is likely to have more of an economic motive and to be less under the influence of strong emotion.' She smiled. 'Anyway, that's how it strikes me.'

'In effect, you're ruling out Farmer.'

'Not necessarily. After all he can be bitter and spiteful, but still have economic gain as his chief motive. It's a question of proportions. All I'm saying is that a demand for a hundred thousand pounds points to someone who is more practical than otherwise.'

'The awful part is that Sipson is going to get off once the jury know that a similar scheme has been perpetrated while he's been in Brixton prison. They can't possibly convict him in those circumstances.'

'Whoever is behind the Swallow Sugar demand obviously knew every detail of Sipson's operation. I mean the letters are virtually identical.'

'What's more, I bet we hear tomorrow that they were typed on the same machine.'

'It does very much look as if you've got the wrong man in the dock,' Clare said, giving Nick a rueful glance. 'I know you still believe he's guilty, but how much are you persuaded by your knowledge of his previous convictions for blackmail?'

'A lot.'

'And if you think about it, he's made no admissions and he has given an explanation of sorts for the various items of evidence that appear to incriminate him.'

'And what explanations! If you were on the jury, would you believe what he says about finding the key beneath his seat and intending to hand it in at the box office when he left but forgetting because he'd come over faint; would you believe that?'

'It does stretch credulity a bit. Incidentally, where was he living at the time of his arrest?'

'He had a basement room off the Old Brompton Road.'

'Does that mean that South Kensington Station was on his way home?'

'Yes.'

'How long had he lived there?'

'Not long. Two or three weeks I think.'

'And where did he live before then?'

'I've no idea. Why?'

'I just wondered.'

'What were you just wondering?'

'Whether you'd like what's left of the apricot flan or would sooner have cheese?'

'It's not fair to pump me and then turn all mysterious and change the subject.'

Clare leaned over and took his hand. 'I'm not trying to be mysterious, Nick. I was only following up a line of thought.'

'So what was your line of thought?'

'Just that Herbert Sipson sounds a bit of a loner. No family, no friends, no anchors of any sort.'

'He has a sister-in-law,' Nick said, in an uninterested tone, as he got up and took his plate over to the sink. He returned to the table bearing the apricot flan.

'Are you going to be at the Old Bailey tomorrow?' Clare asked.

'I doubt it. I imagine Wilcox will want me with him.'

'I hope you're there when the judge gives Sipson a copy of the letter sent to Swallow Sugar. I'd love to see his expression.'

'I'll observe and report on it.'

'It could tell one a great deal.'

49

'It burns me up that he's got to be given it,' Nick said vehemently.

'It would be grossly unfair not to disclose it to him.'

'Oh, I know all that. But if you'd had anything to do with our Herbert, you'd understand, too. He's as phoney as they come. He's a vicious little crook beneath all that ingratiating manner.'

'I'd still like to see him for myself.'

'He'd curdle your milk in advance.'

Clare giggled. Getting up, she came round the table and kissed Nick on the bridge of his nose.

'You've got me really intrigued. While you're snoring, I shall lie awake thinking about it, Master Attwell being anti-sleep at the moment.'

'Stirring is he?'

'Pounding the beat is more like it.'

CHAPTER FOUR

Herbert stepped into the dock the next morning and looked about him with the same bright, expectant air, after first making his small bows to the judge and the jury.

Two middle-aged women on the jury gave him furtive smiles, which he boldly acknowleged.

'You may be seated,' Mr Justice Tidyman said sharply, observing with distaste the exchange of smiles. 'Yes, Mr Vane, your next witness.'

From where he sat in the well of the Court, Nick could see only Herbert's head and shoulders over the top of the front edge of the dock. He noticed him scan the public gallery and he looked up there himself. There didn't appear to be anyone attempting to communicate with Herbert by sign language, but Herbert continued to gaze intently around him as though looking for someone.

It was not until the first witness of the day had made his way to the box that Herbert focused his attention on the next stage of his trial.

The witness came from the Metropolitan Police Laboratory and testified that the letter received by the Shangri-La Bingo Company could have been typed on an Olivetti portable typewriter.

'*Could* have been?' Herbert asked triumphantly when invited to cross-examine.

'Yes, could have been,' the witness replied in a dispassionate tone.

'So you can't say for certain?'

'I've already made that clear.'

'Why can't you?'

'Because I've not examined the machine on which the letter is supposed to have been typed.'

'Do you know that I don't own a typewriter?'

'Really!' the judge exploded. 'How can this witness possibly answer that question? He doesn't pretend to know what you own and what you don't own.'

'Anyway, the police have never handed you a typewriter?'

'That's correct.'

'So why do you say it was typed on an Olivetti machine?'

'I said it *could* have been. It's similar. I can't say more than that.'

'And if I tell you ...'

'You will tell him nothing,' the judge broke in. 'I take it you have no further questions to ask the witness?'

'Not if your lordship says so.'

'Do you have any more questions?'

'I can't think of any, my lord.'

'Then you'd better sit down and we'll have the next witness.'

This was a young detective constable who testified to keeping Herbert under observation in the Adonis Cinema, to seeing him move to seat number 8 in the back row as soon as it became vacant and thereafter to seeing him feel beneath the seat as though searching for something.

It was with an air of long-suffering that Mr Justice Tidyman looked towards Herbert as Vane sat down on completion of the witness's examination-in-chief.

'Yes,' he said wearily, watching Herbert spring to life like a dog about to be let off its lead.

'You say you saw me move to seat 8 when it became vacant?'

'I did.'

'Would you agree that I had a better view from there than I had from my first seat?'

'Seat number 8 was more in the centre.'

'So I'd have had a better view?' Herbert persisted, giving the jury a quietly triumphant look.

'Yes.' He paused while Herbert continued to look at the

jury in a satisfied manner. 'But there were other seats with as good a view which had been vacant all the time.'

Herbert's jaw sagged for a moment. 'But were there not people sitting immediately in front of those seats?'

'I don't recall whether there was someone in front of each of the vacant seats in the back row.'

'You don't recall, eh? So isn't it possible I moved to seat 8 because it had the best view of all?'

'Possible, but unlikely.'

Mr Justice Tidyman whose mind had wandered for a brief moment now re-entered the fray. 'This witness can't possibly say why you moved, only that you did move.'

'But he's saying he kept me under close observation and yet he can't say whether the seats in front of all the vacant ones were occupied.'

'That's a comment and not a question. Have you any further questions?'

'Yes, I have, my lord. Shall I go on?'

Mr Justice Tidyman's only answer to this was to remain quite motionless.

'You say you saw me search for something beneath my seat?' Herbert said, turning back to the witness.

'I did.'

'How do you know I was searching for something?'

'Because that's what I saw.'

'But you were four seats away?'

'Yes.'

'And there was someone sitting in between us?'

'Yes.'

'So you couldn't really see what I was doing?'

'I could.'

'Couldn't I have been bending down to pick up my hand-kerchief?'

'No.'

'Are you positive and certain?'

'Well, it didn't look like that. It looked as if you were feeling beneath the seat.'

'But you can't be sure?'

'I've said what I saw,' the witness said, woodenly.

'But you might have been mistaken?'

'I don't think so.'

Herbert pulled out a handkerchief and wiped his forehead which was glistening with beads of perspiration.

In the pause that followed, the judge said, 'Let me get this clear, Mr Sipson. Are you suggesting to this witness that you never searched for anything beneath your seat?'

'Yes, because I didn't.'

'But, as I understand it, the key was later found in your possession. Are you disputing that?'

'Oh, no, my lord. But I never deliberately searched for it like this officer says. I just happened to feel it as my hand came up from picking up my handkerchief.'

'Yes, I follow,' the judge said in a tone of impeccable neutrality. 'Does that complete your cross-examination?'

'Yes, my lord.'

'He didn't do that badly,' Vane remarked in an aside to his junior.

'He's got poor old Tidyman almost punch-drunk, even though he is supposed to be the referee.'

'Don't worry, judges always come out on top in the end.'

The next witness was Nick Attwell who gave evidence of having seen Herbert leave the cinema, of having followed and kept him under observation and of finally arresting him and taking part in his interrogation at the police station.

He turned to face Herbert's cross-examination with considerably greater equanimity than he usually felt at this juncture. He never went into the witness-box without experiencing butterflies in his tummy and cross-examination *could* be a real test of one's nerve. It was no good saying that the truthful witness could not be disconcerted, for he most certainly could be. And if, as quite often, the truth had to be trimmed and hedged to a certain extent, then you really had to have your wits about you. It didn't mean you were trying to mislead the

Court, but simply that you were obliged to keep within the confines of the rules of evidence.

'Would you say I looked ill when I left the cinema that evening?' Herbert now asked, with a hopeful smile.

'No-o, I wouldn't say you looked ill.'

'Did I not hurry out?'

'Yes.'

'Did you notice me take a deep breath when I got into the fresh air?'

'No.'

'But you're not saying I didn't?'

'No.'

'And did I look ill on the train between Piccadilly and South Kensington?'

'You put your hand to your forehead quite often.'

'As though I had a headache?'

'Could have been.'

'Why else should I have done that?'

Throwing the judge a hasty glance, Herbert added, 'Perhaps the witness can't answer that, my lord.'

'You took the words right out of my mouth, Mr Sipson.'

Herbert smiled delightedly. A smile which he then turned on the jury as though to ensure they didn't feel left out of anything.

'You can't say that I wasn't feeling ill, can you?'

'No. I can only say how you appeared.'

'And from my appearance I might have been feeling ill, mightn't I?'

'Mr Sipson, this is not a profitable line of questioning,' Mr Justice Tidyman remarked with a sigh. 'In any event, you have now made your point, so will you please pass on to another topic, if you have one.'

Herbert nodded eagerly as if to indicate his full agreement with the judge.

'I was very surprised when you stopped and questioned me, wasn't I?' Herbert said, turning again in Nick's direction.

'No, I wouldn't have said you were surprised.'

'What was I then?'

'It struck me most that you were composed.'

'Composed?' the judge said, with a slight frown. 'Do you mean as opposed to agitated or alarmed?'

'Yes, my lord.'

'The very reverse of surprised in fact?' the judge went on.

'Yes, my lord.'

'I follow. Yes, you may continue, Mr Sipson.'

'But I was surprised, wasn't I?' Herbert said.

'The witness has just said that you didn't appear to him to be so.'

'But how can he say that when surprise was written all over my face?'

'He has given his answer and you must accept it unless he wishes to alter it.'

'Do you wish to alter it?' Herbert enquired anxiously.

'No.'

'Next question,' Mr Justice Tidyman said quickly.

'And then you searched me in a shop doorway, didn't you?' Herbert asked, making it sound as though he'd been subjected to a particularly nauseous indignity.

'Yes. That's when we found the key.'

'And I was surprised, wasn't I?'

'You explained that you had meant to hand it in at the box office when you left the cinema.'

'And I'd forgotten?'

'That's what you said.'

'Did you believe me when I said that?'

The judge made a motion with his hand as though holding up a line of traffic.

'It doesn't matter whether he believed you or not. He's here to give evidence of facts, not beliefs.'

'If you say so, my lord.'

'I do.'

'And then you took me to the police station and questioned me, hoping I'd break down and confess?'

'No.'

'You mean that you hoped I *wouldn't* confess?' Herbert asked, gathering the jury up in a look that caused Nick to flush, though he hoped not too obviously. He was annoyed with himself for falling for such a clear heads-I-win-tails-you-lose sort of question.

'What I mean,' he said stolidly, 'is that nothing was done to break you down, as you put it, nor did we try and get you to confess. It was made clear that it was entirely a matter for you whether you said anything or not.'

'Was I not told that I'd be kept there until I did confess?'

'No.'

'Don't you remember Mr Lapham telling me that it would make things much easier for me if I confessed?'

'Certainly not.'

'You don't remember that?' Herbert's air was that of someone whose faith in human goodness had received a fatal clout.

'I don't remember it because it was never said,' Nick replied firmly.

'Tch, tch,' Herbert said, shaking his head slowly from side to side. 'Anyway, I didn't confess, did I?'

'No.'

'In fact, I denied all knowledge of any blackmail scheme?'

'You did.'

'And went on doing so despite the pressure to make what would have been a false confession?'

'No pressure was put on you.'

Mr Justice Tidyman who had refrained from intervention for some time now felt obliged to speak.

'You have made your point sufficiently often to leave it. In due course you will have an opportunity of telling the jury your own version of all these events. In the meantime, confine yourself to questions and avoid disputacious observations.'

'Then I have nothing further to ask this witness,' Herbert said in a tone of umbrage and sat down, at the same time casting a covert look at the jury.

It was during the luncheon adjournment, which came a little later, that the judge sent for Philip Vane and outlined his plan for the future course of the trial.

'It has occurred to me,' he said after inviting counsel to sit down, 'that it won't be sufficient merely to exclude the jury when I hand a copy of this other blackmail letter to the accused. I'm bound to go into an explanation of sorts and the temptation to the press to publish something of this threat to the nation's sugar supplies will be overwhelming even though they are normally careful not to print anything which occurs in the course of the trial in the absence of the jury. I just can't take a chance in this instance and I'm certainly not prepared to take the responsibility for creating a national panic over contaminated sugar. I've therefore decided to deal with the matter in chambers which means that press and public can be excluded. How does that strike you?'

'I think it's a very good idea, judge.'

'My next proposal is not to sit on Monday which will give the police a bit more time to investigate the new threat before our trial reaches too advanced a stage. Does that course also commend itself to you?'

'That, too, is an excellent idea, judge.'

'Finally, when we resume the trial next Tuesday, which is a crucial day in the Swallow Sugar affair, I might decide to go into camera. It'll create a furore of speculation, but I can't help that.'

'On what grounds would you do that, judge? The requirements of public interest?'

'In the interests of public safety. The more I've thought about it, the more appalled I've become at the nature of the threat to Swallow Sugar. It is obviously of vital importance that no word of it is made known until after the threat has passed. Anyway, that's what I'm contemplating, though I shan't make a final decision until Tuesday morning. I shall be grateful if you will supply me with up-to-date information before we sit.'

'Certainly, judge.'

Mr Justice Tidyman sighed. 'What an odious crime black-mail is! And no less so because it has become highly fashion-able.'

CHAPTER FIVE

Sir Arnold Swallow sat with a grim, drawn expression. There was a faint rime round his lips.

His cousin, Ralph Swallow, also wore a grave expression, though to Nick it looked more assumed than natural. As if he felt he had to try and match his chairman's strained appearance.

Detective Chief Superintendent Wilcox had picked Nick up at the Old Bailey soon after he had finished giving evidence and now they were closeted in Sir Arnold's office at Swallow House.

The fifth person present was the personnel director, who had been introduced as Sandy Tarring and who had arrived in the room bearing a batch of folders.

These, he explained, were the records of employees who had been given the sack during the past year and who might conceivably, therefore, have nurtured a grievance against the company.

The five men sat round a conference table at one end of Sir Arnold's spacious office.

'There surely must be something more we can do,' Sir Arnold said in a tight voice. 'We can't just sit around and twiddle our thumbs for the next three days.'

'There's precious little we can do until the blackmailer makes contact,' Wilcox observed. 'And that won't be before next Tuesday at the earliest. Not that the police are going to be inactive,' he added. 'We've already arranged to monitor all telephone calls and that means your private calls at home as well, Sir Arnold. And, of course, we're doing our best to trace Farmer. With any luck, we'll have news of him over the weekend.'

'I still think he could be behind this,' Ralph Swallow said.

'He's certainly a more likely suspect than anyone in this lot,' Tarring remarked, tapping the pile of folders.

'We shall want to check on those,' Wilcox said. 'Nothing can be left to chance.'

'I hardly slept last night,' Sir Arnold remarked in a tone which showed he had not been listening to what the others had been saying. 'I was haunted by the thought of innocent persons being exposed to danger by our sugar. It's the biggest crisis the company has ever faced and it seems we're powerless to deal with it. All we can do is wait on some madman's whim.'

'Once the fellow makes contact, things'll move quickly enough,' Ralph Swallow said in a tone of robust reassurance.

'How do we know there aren't already bags of contaminated sugar on some supermarket shelves?'

'I think the answer to that, Sir Arnold, is that we don't, but it's unlikely. If the blackmailer's main object is to relieve you of £100,000, he's not going to put his threat into operation until he thinks you're just stringing him along and have no intention of paying up.'

'But supposing he's already found out we've contacted the police?'

'How could he have?' Wilcox asked sharply, looking from one to other of the three directors.

'Certainly not from here,' Ralph Swallow said.

'Nor from our side,' Wilcox said. 'We've taken every precaution to avoid any leaks.'

'The three of us here and Sir Arnold's secretary are the only people in the whole of Swallow House to be aware of what's happening.'

Sir Arnold appeared to emerge once more from his state of withdrawal.

'We've been thinking only in terms of ex-employees who might have a grievance against the Company, but what about our existing staff? Oughtn't we to check on them?'

'I don't see how we can do that,' Tarring said, 'without making enquiries at shop-floor level and that'll inevitably spark off rumours. After all we employ over five thousand people.'

Wilcox took off his spectacles and tapped his teeth in a thoughtful manner with one of the outstretched arms.

'Supposing one of your employees was voicing a grievance, would you expect to hear about it?' he asked.

'Probably not. It would depend on what he said and who overheard it and whether it was taken seriously. For example, if someone was overheard saying he intended planting a bomb in the refinery and it was believed that he really might, obviously the matter would be reported. At least, I would sincerely hope so. In a work-force the size of ours, one's bound to have a few misfits, a few oddities, and they are the sort in whom a grudge could quietly fester without anyone being aware of the fact.'

'Hmm. Would it be possible for you to provide me with a list of such people without exciting attention?'

Tarring pursed his lips. 'I suppose it could be done through the various managers. I could think up some pretext for wanting the information.'

'You could say you wanted it for social research purposes,' Ralph Swallow said.

Tarring nodded. 'I'll think of some reason.'

'That would be helpful,' Wilcox said. He glanced round the table. 'If I need to contact any of you gentlemen over the weekend, I take it I can get you at your home numbers which I have?' They nodded in turn. 'And if you want to get in touch with me, you have my extension number at the Yard which you can dial direct without going through the switchboard. There'll be someone manning the phone day and night.' He rose from his chair. 'If not before, I'll be in touch with you first thing on Monday morning, Sir Arnold.'

Sir Arnold Swallow gave a preoccupied nod. 'I don't think I have ever in my whole life looked forward less to a weekend,' he said grimly.

As they were driving away from Swallow House, Wilcox

remarked, 'Bit like a Presbyterian funeral in there, wasn't it?'

Nick grinned. 'Odd thing is that I'd have expected Sir Arnold to be the tough one of the family. But he seems to have taken it much harder than Ralph Swallow.'

'He's older and he *is* the head of the company, so his feeling of responsibility is probably the greater. I agree he looks one of those incisive captains of industry, but it just shows that you can't always judge by appearances. He was almost pathetic this afternoon. I suppose the full horror of the situation had had time to sink in.'

They drove in silence for a time and then Nick said, 'If it's all right, sir, I'd like to get back to the Old Bailey for the last half hour. I'd like to be there when the judge hands Sipson a copy of the Swallow letter.'

'I fully intend we should both be there,' Wilcox said. 'Incidentally, I didn't tell you that we've had a preliminary lab report on the letter. It could have been typed on the same machine as the other, but they can't say for certain. They've got further tests to make. Unfortunately, if it was the same machine, it was one without any peculiarities, which makes it that much less easy to identify.'

When they arrived at the Old Bailey, the judge was just telling the jury that he proposed to adjourn early as he had a matter to deal with in chambers and, furthermore, that the Court would not be sitting on Monday. He regretted any inconvenience this might cause, but something unforeseen had occurred to preclude the continuation of the trial that day.

From their generally bovine expressions, the jury had no particular feelings either way. As they filed out of their seats, Herbert watched them for the opportunity of exchanging a smile. Given a chance, Nick reflected, and he'll be leaning over to shake hands like a politician on a whistle-stop tour.

Mr Justice Tidyman sat back in his chair idly watching the departing figures. One or two pressmen were whispering urgently to the usher who was trying to shoo them out. One finally turned round and called out to the judge.

'My lord, surely the press are allowed to remain in Court?'

'I fear not,' Mr Justice Tidyman said in his most courteous voice. 'A chambers sitting is always in private.'

Muttering indignantly, the *Daily Chronicle*'s man departed through the swing doors at the back.

When he was satisfied that the Court had been cleared, the judge addressed himself to Herbert, who sat waiting in the dock with an expression of ill-suppressed expectation rather like a dog who senses that the moment for a walk is about to be declared.

'I want you to listen to me carefully, Sipson,' Mr Justice Tidyman began in a judicial tone.

'Yes, my lord,' Herbert put in eagerly.

'And not interrupt.' Herbert seemed about to give this assurance, but remained silent when the judge held up an admonitory hand. 'Since your trial began yesterday, a document has come into the possession of the crown which could be relevant to the defence you are putting forward. Normally, prosecuting counsel would have supplied a copy of this document to your counsel for such use as he saw fit to make of it in your defence. However, as you are not represented by counsel, the prosecution has very properly made me aware of the position and I am about to hand the document to you. I want you to read it and then I shall have further words to say on the subject. I do *not* want you to make any comment at all yourself. Is that understood?'

'Yes, your lordship,' Herbert replied, his face shining with anticipation. 'I'm sorry, your lordship, but you must excuse me. I'm ...' His voice faltered.

'Just calm yourself. Usher, take this to the accused, please.'

The usher handed the letter to Herbert who took it with trembling fingers.

He appeared to read it with breathless speed. Then passing his tongue quickly across his lips, he looked up.

'I've read it, my lord,' he said in a voice tight with emotion.

'Very well, now listen to me again. You will have noted that there are similarities between that letter and the one which was sent to the Shangri-La Bingo Company.' Herbert nodded vigorously. 'They are such that it could be suggested that both letters must have been written by the same person.'

'I've always said I was innocent,' Herbert burst out.

'I asked you not to interrupt,' the judge said coldly.

'I'm sorry, your lordship, but ...'

'Be quiet until I tell you that you may speak. When the time comes for you to make your defence, you may, under my guidance, use that document to indicate to the jury your innocence of the charges against you.' The judge's tone became more severe as he went on, 'In the meantime, you are not to show the document to any person, nor are you to discuss it with anyone. I shall give instructions to the prison authorities to ensure that my injunction is observed. Finally, let me say this, when the trial resumes on Tuesday, I shall not tolerate any reference to the document in Court without your first seeking my direction. Now, is there anything you wish to say before the Court adjourns?'

Herbert clutched the front of the dock with both hands and said in a ringing tone, 'I hope, my lord, that you will consider it your duty to stop my trial. I have all along proclaimed my innocence and this letter proves it. I think you should tell the prosecution to drop the case, my lord. That is all I wish to say. I thank you, my lord.'

He was in the process of giving the judge a deep bow when Mr Justice Tidyman rose and, without further word, briskly left the bench.

'Well,' Philip Vane said, his head cocked on one side as he looked at the three police officers standing in front of him, 'what did you make of that little exhibition?'

'A load of old theatricals,' Lapham observed in a disgusted tone. 'There isn't one genuine emotion in the man.'

'Is that your view, too, Mr Wilcox?' counsel enquired.

'It's the first time I've seen Sipson, Mr Vane. I'm keeping an open mind for the time being,' Wilcox replied, delicately stroking the bridge of his spectacles.

'And what about you, Sergeant Attwell?'

'I don't know where the truth lies, sir, but I'm sure Sipson could tell everyone a lot more if he wanted to.'

'And what is *your* view?' Wilcox asked.

Vane puffed out his cheeks and then slowly deflated them.

'I'm damned if I know,' he said, with an explosive laugh. 'I feel I've witnessed a rather clever trick, but have absolutely no idea how it was done.'

'The trouble with lawyers,' Lapham said later as they were on their way back to the Yard, 'is that they see too many bloody sides to everything.'

'It's their training that makes them detached, Fred,' Wilcox remarked.

'I daresay it is, but I don't want detached barristers handling my cases. I want fully committed ones.' He let out an angry snort. 'Anyone who saw Sipson that evening he walked into the trap we'd prepared knows he's guilty. And there are no two ways about it. Guilty: g-u-i-l-t-y; if that's how it's still spelt.'

Wilcox laughed, while Nick decided he had best keep his head below the parapet. He had no desire to draw any of his guvnor's fire on himself. Lapham was obviously in a raw mood as a result of what had happened in Court.

When they arrived back at the Yard, Wilcox instructed Nick to phone Minnie Dove at *The Three Ducks* and enquire whether there had been any news of Farmer.

'But no point in doing so before half past seven,' he added. 'If he's there, we'll phone the local station to keep tabs on him, while we get out to Heston as fast as a car can take us.'

It was nearer to twenty to eight when Nick did make the call. A male voice answered and he asked to speak to Mrs Dove. He tried to recall whether he had seen a telephone when he had been there the previous evening. There was a distant, muffled sound of voices and he imagined the phone must be in some private part of the premises.

It was a full two minutes before he heard the receiver being picked up and a voice said, 'Mrs Dove speaking, who is that?'

'Good evening, Mrs Dove, you may remember my colleague and I were talking to you last night.'

'Oh, were you the ones from the insurance company?'

'That's right.'

'You were asking about Mr Farmer?'

'That's right. I just wondered whether you happened to have heard from him today?'

'As a matter of fact, I have. Not exactly from him, but of him. I gather he's gone away. Called away suddenly to a sick relative.'

'Do you know where?'

'\'Fraid not. Apparently he had to pack up in a hurry and go.'

'Whom did you hear this from?'

'Somebody phoned me. I don't know who it was. Just said he had a message for me from Mr Farmer and that was it.'

'A man?'

'A man? What, Mr Farmer?'

'No, the person who phoned.'

'Oh, I'm sorry. Yes, it was a man.'

'And you didn't recognise the voice?'

'No. He was a complete stranger as far as I was concerned.'

'Thank you, Mrs Dove. Thank you for your help.'

'Not at all, you're welcome. Look in again sometime.'

'Sure. Good-night.'

It was later, much later when Nick was in bed and drifting into sleep and Clare said suddenly in a very wide-awake voice, 'I wonder if there's any connection between Farmer and Shangri-La Bingo Company.'

CHAPTER SIX

It was during exercise on Saturday that Herbert became aware that he was the object of special observation.

He had fallen into step with a prisoner named Butcher who was awaiting trial for forgery and who had been outlining to Herbert a new foolproof credit card swindle, details of which he now claimed to have perfected. They had completed only two circuits of the yard when the officer in charge told them to break it up. Later as they were returning to the cell block, Butcher closed in beside Herbert and told him in a puzzled tone that the officer had wanted to know what they had been talking about, in particular what Herbert had said in the course of their conversation.

'You been up to something?' Butcher enquired out of the side of his mouth.

'Not that I know of,' Herbert replied, flashing his companion a smile.

And then later in the day, during recreation, there was further evidence that he was being specially watched. It came while he was playing draughts with a prisoner of the name of Japp. Herbert had an inordinate passion for the game at which he was rather good so that he usually won. This was sufficient to put off most people after one or two games. But the patient Japp didn't seem to mind losing and had thus become Herbert's regular nightly opponent. While Herbert's pieces leap-frogged about the board eliminating Japp's the two men would exchange news of their day's happenings.

On this Saturday evening, they had scarcely begun playing

when a prison officer sidled over and stood at their side.

'Hoping to pick up a few hints?' Herbert asked, cheerfully.

'That's right. You're pretty good, aren't you, Sipson?'

'I reckon I can hold my own.'

'He can beat me all right,' Japp said.

'So I've noticed. Do you ever win?'

'Not so far.'

'Why do you go on then?'

Japp looked up and frowned. 'What's winning or losing got to do with it?'

'I'd get bored if I always lost. I'd want to do something else after a time.' He paused. 'But perhaps it's Sipson's company you enjoy. His sparkling conversation.'

Herbert smiled quietly to himself as he removed two more of Japp's pieces and claimed a king.

'How's your trial going?' the officer asked when neither of them had responded to his previous observation.

'You'd better ask the eight women on the jury,' Herbert said, smiling again.

'Eight! How'd you fix that?'

'I didn't fix anything. It was the way it happened.'

'You're lucky you're not on a rape charge. They'd have your pelt for a lampshade.'

'If I had been on a rape charge,' Herbert said with dignity, 'I'd have challenged them.'

'Quite a little lawyer, aren't you? As it is, I suppose you're winning them over?'

'We'll see.'

'I reckon you could be quite a ladies' man, Sipson.'

'You could be right.'

'Married are you?'

'No.'

'Ran off, did she?'

'If I'd ever had a wife, she wouldn't have run off.'

'Just listen to that for manly confidence!'

'I sometimes wish my old woman would run off,' Japp said, gloomily. 'Instead of which, she's always visiting and telling me what a rotten husband I am. Which I know, anyway.'

'What's your trouble?'

'I nicked a couple of bottles of Scotch.'

'Couldn't you have had that dealt with in the magistrates' court?'

'They refused. I pleaded guilty, but they've sent me up the road for sentence.'

'Oh, you've been inside for it before, have you?'

Japp glanced up at the officer and sniffed.

'I reckon I served my first sentence while you were still pissing over anyone who had you on their lap.'

'He still does,' a voice called out behind them.

The officer swung round, but only to see a row of backs of those watching television. At that moment he was called over to the door to speak to another officer.

'Funny that you've never got married,' Japp remarked, as Herbert set the pieces out for another game.

'Why?'

'I agree with what that screw said about your looking a bit of a ladies' man.'

'Oh, I'm not saying I couldn't have got married,' Herbert said, archly.

'God, you're starting another game, are you?' the officer said, returning to their side.

'I thought you were interested in seeing how it's done,' Herbert observed.

'I am, I am.'

'Well, watch this,' he added, hopping over three of Japp's pieces in an aggressive foray, while Japp looked on with a worried frown.

'Where'd you learn to play?'

'As a kid with my brother. He was older than me and I used to lose in those days.'

'Where's he now?'

'My brother? I lost touch with him about five years ago after his wife died. He sold up and drifted up north.'

'What about the rest of your family?'

'I only had one brother.'

'I had two older brothers. They both used to give me hell as a kid.'

'Is that why you're now a screw?' Japp asked.

'What's that supposed to mean?'

'Now you like taking it out of others.'

'Your humour's on a par with your draughts, Japp.'

'He was bloody nosey tonight,' Japp remarked, as they prepared to return to their cells.

Herbert nodded. There was no doubt that orders had gone out not only to watch him, but to take every opportunity of pumping him as well; and there could be only one explanation of that. It was to do with that letter the judge had handed him and which lay folded in his coat pocket. Indeed, the judge had talked about certain instructions being given to the prison authorities to ensure he didn't disclose it to anyone. Well, they need not worry because he had no intention of doing so. But if they wanted to waste their time and energies watching over him, that was their concern. He refused to allow it even to spoil his sessions of draughts with Japp.

Some time later, after lights out, he was lying on his un-yielding bed gazing up at the ceiling. His hands were clasped behind his head and he was smiling in the dark. Suddenly a thought struck him. It crept into his mind from nowhere, but its effect was first to freeze his smile and then slowly erase it from his features.

CHAPTER SEVEN

Farmer looked about his new room and nodded with satisfaction.

'Yes, this'll do me very nicely,' he said, turning to the
landlady who stood in the doorway.

'It's £5 a week, payable in advance. And, of course, that
doesn't include any meals.'

'No, of course not.' He extracted a £5 note from his wallet
and handed it to her.

'You didn't tell me your name.'

'Farmer. Jeffrey Farmer. Jeffrey spelt with a J.'

'Are you likely to be late in? If so, I'll give you a key.
Perhaps I'd better, anyway. But please don't go and lose it,'
she added in a voice which indicated that her lodgers were
prone to do this.

'I don't expect to be late,' he said, 'but it would be helpful
to have a key and then I needn't disturb anyone. I'm sure
I shan't lose it.'

'You won't be having visitors up in your room, will you?'
she asked in a tone that allowed only one answer.

'No, most certainly not. I have a lot of paper work to get
through and it was the quiet look of your house that attracted
me to it. Visitors are the last thing I want.'

She glanced at his upturned typewriter in its case. 'You
don't use that thing late at night, I hope,' she said. He shook
his head. 'Well, I'll leave you to unpack, Mr Farmer,' she
went on. 'The bathroom and toilet are situated on the half-
landing. There's a charge of 15p for a bath as I have to switch

on the immersion heater. You won't want one this evening, will you?'

'No.'

She departed, closing the bedroom door behind her and Farmer walked across to the window and looked out. He had a view of the narrow strip of garden which ran from the back of the house to a paling fence which divided it and the neighbouring gardens from a cemetery.

He returned to the bed and sat down. Yes, he felt distinctly pleased with his choice.

When he had decided that it would be prudent to get away from Heston, he had first thought of moving himself into a neighbouring borough. But then it had come to him that it would be better to put rather more distance than that between himself and Heston. There was also the advantage of moving into a different police area.

And so he had come to Reading which was not too far away and yet far enough for him to feel secure from detection. And in Reading, he had found just the right sort of room, both quiet and central.

He picked up the folded newspaper which he had bought for his train journey and opened it up at the page which contained a large advertisement for Swallow Sugar. The text, which was encircled by soaring and diving swallows, reminded the reader of the great and vital part played by Swallow Sugar Corporation in the nation's life. For several seconds, Farmer stared at the advertisement with an expression of growing disdain. Then suddenly holding the page up in front of him, he jabbed a vicious finger through the paper and ripped it from top to bottom. Afterwards he wiped his feet on the torn page as it lay on the floor.

Taking out his wallet once more, he extracted all the money and slowly counted it. There was £55, which represented his total wealth. It was all that remained of his severance pay when Swallow Sugar had unceremoniously dismissed him.

He replaced the notes carefully in his wallet and slowly

unpacked his few belongings. By the time he had finished, it was seven o'clock and he decided to go out and have supper. He had noticed a café about a quarter of a mile away where he'd have a meat pie and a mug of tea. Then, depending how he felt, he might find a pub and have a pint of beer. It wouldn't be like *The Three Ducks*, though, where he could talk to people, especially people like Minnie Dove who was a real friend, always sympathetic and helpful.

In the event, he decided he was not in the mood to go drinking, so after he'd had his supper, he took a short stroll before returning to his room and lying on top of the bed.

The stroll had also fulfilled the purpose of a reconnaissance. He was able to take note of the nearest newsagent's shop and of the telephone kiosk.

Tomorrow would be Sunday and he would not get up till lunchtime. He hoped that Miss Whatever-her-name-was had no rules about lying in on a Sunday morning.

He had not enquired her name and she had not volunteered it. On the other hand, she had asked him his and he had given it to her.

He couldn't help wondering now whether he would not have been better advised to have given a false one.

CHAPTER EIGHT

Sir Arnold Swallow always got up at half past six and Sundays were no exception.

But whereas on working days he would be in his office soon after nine o'clock, on Sundays he would at the same hour be on the first tee of the golf course which lay about five miles from his home.

He and a local doctor and a couple of other men made up a regular foursome.

On this particular Sunday, however, he had been sorely tempted to phone his friends and cry off. He just wasn't in the mood for golf or for their company. He had had another bad night and the heavy black cloud of worry which hung over his head seemed, if anything, to have intensified.

Finally, it was his wife, to whom he had at the outset confided the cause of his anxiety, who persuaded him to go and play.

'It'll do you good to get out,' she had said. 'If you stay around the house, you'll only brood and feel worse.' All of which he recognised as being true.

So it was that he and his three companions found themselves on the first tee as usual. On this occasion he and John Lindley, the doctor, were paired together.

It fell to Sir Arnold to drive off and he hooked the ball into the rough on the left of the fairway. As their opponent then promptly sliced his ball, the two couples immediately parted company and made off in their different directions.

'Not like you to hook, Arnold,' Lindley said. 'Never known you go off the fairway at the first before.'

Sir Arnold grunted and they walked the rest of the way in silence to where the ball lay nestling against a particularly large tuft of coarse grass. Dr Lindley managed to chip it back on to the fairway, only to have his partner play another bad shot and land the ball in a deep bunker to the left of the green.

'It's certainly not your day,' Lindley remarked with a dry smile.

'Sorry about those two shots,' Sir Arnold said gruffly. 'Fact is I'm feeling a bit off colour.'

'I thought as much. I noticed you looked a bit drawn and puffy round the eyes. And your golf confirms. What's the trouble?'

'Oh, we've got some trouble in the company.'

'Surely there's nothing new in that situation?'

'I suppose not,' Sir Arnold said in an abstracted tone. 'It's just that some problems are more intractable than others.'

'Whose are not? Anyway, like me to give you a check-up?'

'I'll think about it.'

'Don't think about it for too long, that's all.'

'Oh, good lord, I'm not about to die or anything like that.'

Dr Lindley looked at his partner with a mildly quizzical expression. 'Probably not, though it hardly lies with you to say so. If there is anything the matter with you, the sooner it's diagnosed the better.'

'It's just a small dose of common-or-garden worry,' Sir Arnold remarked with a wan smile.

'You've never struck me as being the worrying type.'

'I normally hide it better, that's all.' His tone was dismissive and Dr Lindley gave a small shrug, as he veered off to clamber into the bunker in which their ball was resting.

During the next three holes, the four of them kept fairly well together, but at the fifth, their paths diverged again and Sir Arnold and Dr Lindley set off to search for their ball which Sir Arnold had driven into a small coppice.

'There was something I was going to ask you, John,' Sir

Arnold said in a studiedly casual voice. 'Nothing whatsoever to do with my condition,' he added with a thin smile. 'What exactly is the effect of ground glass on the system?'

Dr Lindley stopped abruptly in his tracks and stared in astonishment at his partner's back.

'You mean if you ingest the stuff?' he enquired, catching Sir Arnold up again.

'Yes. Supposing you swallow some by mistake, what does it do to you?'

'As with most things, it depends who you are and how much you swallow. But it's certainly not something I'd recommend.'

'I daresay not, but you haven't told me what the effect would be.'

'Well, depending on how much you ingested, it would cause more or less damage to your duodenum, to your intestines, to your bowel. In fact, to almost every part of you from your throat downwards. But the worst effects would be to the parts I've mentioned.'

'You'd have a pretty bad pain?'

'An excruciating pain. There'd be inflammation and probably perforations as well in those areas on which the stuff worked.'

'So it could be fatal, too?'

'Yes, though that would obviously depend on the amount in the system.'

Sir Arnold nodded vaguely with a grim expression on his face.

'Why the interest?' Dr Lindley asked.

'Oh, I just wondered. I was reading a book in which one of the characters swallowed some and it didn't seem to me that the author described the symptoms very convincingly.'

'What did he say about them?'

'Oh ... look, there's our ball,' Sir Arnold exclaimed, pointing at the foot of a small oak tree. 'Wait a moment, I'll get a bit ahead so that I can watch where it goes.'

Dr Lindley observed him with a puzzled frown as Sir Arnold quickly moved thirty yards away before turning and indicating that his partner should play his shot.

During the rest of the round, no further mention was made of Sir Arnold's health or of the effects of ground glass on the human system. Their conversation, such as it was, was kept on a desultory level.

With the game finished, the four men retired to the club-house bar, but after a single gin and tonic, Sir Arnold excused himself and drove home, leaving the others to continue their drinking.

He and his wife lunched alone and had just finished their meal when the telephone rang.

'Shall I go?' Lady Swallow asked.

'I'd prefer to take it,' her husband said, as he had of all telephone calls over the past thirty-six hours.

He walked across the hall to his study and sat down at his desk before lifting the receiver. As soon as he did so he heard the pips which indicated that the call was coming from a public kiosk. With a slight quickening of the pulse, he switched on the recording apparatus which the police had fitted to his telephone.

The pips ceased as the caller inserted a coin and a strange voice said, 'I want to speak to Sir Arnold Swallow.'

'Who is that speaking?' Sir Arnold asked in a constricted voice.

'That is Sir Arnold, isn't it?'

'Who are you and what do you want?'

There was a short chuckle at the other end of the line before the voice said, 'I want your head on a charger, Sir Arnold, that's what I want.'

The next moment the caller had rung off and Sir Arnold's ear was mocked by the infuriating persistence of the dialling tone.

His wife looked up with a worried expression as he returned to the dining-room.

'Who was it?'

'Some crank or other.'

'Oughtn't you to tell the police?'

'I'll phone them as soon as we're finished. There's nothing they can do about it.'

'How do you know?'

'Short of catching the man still in the kiosk, there is nothing they can do. And even if he was making the call from the public box in the village, which is utterly unlikely, he won't have hung around. He might have been phoning from anywhere. Now that you can dial almost any part of the country from any other part, calls are not as traceable as they used to be.'

'I still think you should let the police know immediately. After all, that's what you promised to do.'

Sir Arnold popped a last piece of crispbread and cheese into his mouth and got up.

'I'll go and phone them now,' he said in an unusually submissive tone.

The officer at Scotland Yard who answered his call said that he would let Detective Chief Superintendent Wilcox know at once and that Sir Arnold could expect someone to call him back within the next twenty minutes.

As things turned out, the officer was unable to get an immediate reply from Wilcox's number and so phoned Nick Attwell instead.

Nick, who had been just about to begin his own midday meal, agreed to call Sir Arnold straight away and Clare quietly returned their food to the oven. Having been a police officer herself, she'd had none of the customary difficulties of adjustment when she became the wife of one.

'Sir Arnold Swallow? This is Detective Sergeant Attwell speaking. I understand you received a phone call a short time ago? I'd like to hear the details.' When Sir Arnold had finished, Nick said, 'You didn't recognise the voice?'

'No. I would even hazard a guess that it was disguised.'

'Why would he have done that, I wonder, unless you might have recognised it?'

'I'm afraid I can't tell you.'

'Anyway, I'll arrange for the tape to be picked up. Will

there be someone at your home during the rest of the day?'

'I shall be here myself.'

'Thank you for letting us know so promptly. And, of course, if you receive any further calls, get in touch with us again.'

'I will.'

Nick replaced the receiver with a satisfied sigh. 'And now let's have lunch,' he said, turning to Clare with a cheerful smile. 'No need to phone the guvnor till we've eaten.'

'I gather that Sir Arnold Swallow has had a mysterious phone call?' Clare remarked as she put their meal back on the table.

Nick nodded. 'That just about describes it. It sounded like the work of some crank. That's what Sir Arnold himself said.'

'Surely it's more than a coincidence that he should receive such a call at this particular time?'

'Well, it certainly didn't sound like the commercially-motivated blackmailer we're looking for.'

'It might have been part of a softening-up process,' Clare said in a thoughtful tone.

'You mean, to unnerve him so that he's more disposed to give in to the demand when it's finally made?'

'Exactly.'

Nick appeared to give the possibility consideration.

'It's out of pattern with anything that happened in the Sipson case.'

'That doesn't prove anything either way.'

'Agreed. But I still think a coincidence is the more likely bet.'

'Not just *a* coincidence, but a whopping great one,' Clare observed. 'Did you ask Sir Arnold how many anonymous calls of that sort he normally receives at home over a weekend?'

'No. That's a point. I should have done.'

'And I'll wager his answer is none, or as near none as proves my theory.'

'If you're right, the call was made by the person who sent the letter and is trying to squeeze Swallow Sugar for £100,000.'

'Yes.'

'Which rules out Sipson.'

'Ye-s.'

'Well it must do, mustn't it?'

'On the face of it, yes.'

'Oh, come on sweetheart, you can't have it both ways.'

'Have you had time to check whether Farmer was ever connected with the Shangri-La Bingo Company?'

'He wasn't.'

'That's definite, is it?'

'So far as their records go, he never has been, but they have a rapid turnover of staff and I suspect their records mayn't be a hundred per cent accurate. You're getting to be like some T.V. armchair detective, my sweet,' Nick remarked, as he reached forward and speared himself another roast potato.

Clare smiled. 'But without any of the slick solutions, I'm afraid. I find it such an intriguing case. I can't wait for Tuesday.'

'That's certainly going to be the day the kettle boils.'

CHAPTER NINE

As soon as he woke up on Monday morning after a night of uneasy dreaming, Farmer knew that he had to move.

It *had* been a mistake giving his true name to the lady who owned the house. Worse still he had impressed it on her mind by emphasising, as he always did, that his first name was Jeffrey 'spelt with a J'.

It was a pity because in every other way the room suited him admirably. But his personal security must be the prime consideration. He just could not afford to take any risks.

By the time he had finished dressing, he heard the landlady moving about downstairs.

She obviously heard his descent, because she came out of the kitchen as he reached the hall.

'Good morning, Mr Farmer. You're going out now, are you?'

'Only to make a phone call. I'll be back in five or ten minutes.'

If he had required fortifying in his intention, it came in her use of his name when wishing him 'good morning'.

He walked down the street, past the telephone kiosk, and bought a newspaper at the small shop he had noticed on his Saturday evening reconnaissance.

He walked on for a further three or four minutes, then retraced his steps to the house.

He heard sounds of washing-up coming from the kitchen. Tapping on the door, he opened it without waiting for a response.

'I've just had maddening news,' he said, assuming a carefully crestfallen expression. 'I phoned my office and they want me to go up to the Midlands at once. Today. This morning. I'm terribly sorry about the inconvenience.'

'You've paid for a week in advance.'

'I know.'

'I can't make you a full refund, of course, because ... well, you've been here two nights and you've probably stopped me making a further booking for this week.' She stared at him hard as though challenging him to dispute this dubious statement. When he didn't do so, she went on, 'I still have to send your bedlinen to the laundry and they won't charge less because you've only used the sheets two nights.'

'Yes, I realise that.'

'I can't possibly let you have more than a pound back and I'll probably be out of pocket even so.'

She dried her hands on her apron and reached for her handbag which was on the table and took out a £1 note.

'Thank you,' he said, accepting it gratefully. At least it would pay his fare to Oxford which was where he had decided to go.

'Don't forget to give me your key before you leave!'

'Here it is. I'll just go and pack my bag. And again I'm sorry about the inconvenience.'

'I suppose it's not your fault,' she remarked grudgingly, turning back to the sink.

Half an hour later, he was on the station platform waiting for a train.

Once he had made up his mind to move, he'd had no difficulty in deciding on Oxford. It was no great distance away and it had the added advantage of providing the anonymity that went with a large transient population.

And if, by chance, he was sought in Reading, Miss What's-her-name (he still didn't know it) would only be able to say that he had gone to the Midlands, which would mean his pursuers would automatically think in terms of Birmingham and its vicinity.

The train pulled in and Jeffrey Farmer boarded it. When

it reached Oxford, it would be John Butler who got off.

At about the same moment as Farmer alias Butler got on the train, a group of officers gathered in Deputy Assistant Commissioner Napier's room at Scotland Yard.

'I thought it'd be useful to have this con and review events,' the D.A.C. said, 'particularly as you, Fred, and Sergeant Attwell don't have to be at the Old Bailey today.'

Detective Chief Superintendent Lapham, to whom the latter part of the remark was addressed, nodded.

'Before we begin our discussion proper,' the D.A.C. went on, 'I might mention as a matter of interest that I've had a talk with our chief medical adviser on the effects of ground glass on the human system.' He pulled a folded sheet of paper from his jacket pocket. 'These are just a few notes I made. I gather that in practice it is not as dangerous as legend would have us believe. It is not in itself toxic and when swallowed it becomes embedded in the mucous balms of the stomach contents. In theory, one would expect lacerations of the stomach wall and the lower part of the oesophagus, but it doesn't necessarily turn out this way in practice. He pointed out that children often swallow the bitten-off ends of thermometers without ill effects. Obviously, a great deal depends on how much is consumed and even a medium amount could cause vomiting and a nasty stomach ache.' He refolded the sheet of paper. 'Treatment consists of a purgative, and giving the patient lots of bread to increase the amount of material in the stomach.' He looked in turn at the officers sitting round the table. 'What it comes to is this. Even if Mr X does carry out his threat, there won't, given a bit of luck, be any fatalities.'

'In my view,' Wilcox said, 'the psychological effect was always likely to be greater than the physical.'

'I agree, Jack, but I, at least, find a crumb of comfort in the knowledge that the chances of anyone dying are less than we believed. Accepted that, if the public got wind of the threat, the effect would be devastating anyway.'

'I imagine, sir,' Nick said, 'that if you had it in tea or coffee, you might escape harm altogether as it would remain unmelted at the bottom of your cup.'

The D.A.C. nodded. 'There's obviously a far greater risk if it goes into cooking. Cakes and puddings and the like. However, let's now turn to the more pressing aspects of the investigation.' He glanced in Lapham's direction.

'What's the weekend news from Brixton prison, Fred?'

'Nix. Sipson not only didn't have any visitors, but he didn't write any letters. Furthermore, he didn't pass any messages through other prisoners as far as anyone could tell. Oh, and he didn't get any letters either.'

'So he could just as well have spent the weekend on a desert island, eh? Perhaps the judge's admonition really did frighten him into inactivity. The question is whether there's any significance in his lying low. Does it indicate ultra wariness or simple innocence?'

'There's nothing simple nor innocent about that man,' Lapham observed.

'Anyway, the point is that we've learnt nothing from his conduct over the weekend.' He looked towards Wilcox. 'Still no news of Farmer's whereabouts?'

'I'm afraid none. The local police have been making discreet enquiries and can find no trace of him. Mrs Dove at *The Three Ducks* confirms that he's not been back there since Sergeant Attwell and I called.'

'The significant thing there is that Farmer has chosen this particular moment to disappear. Why? It can't be coincidence and if it's not, it must be to do with the demand on Swallow Sugar.'

'As I see it,' Wilcox said, 'he must have guessed that the company would go to the police despite his warning and he would know that his name would very likely come up as a suspect. That would be enough to make him disappear.'

'We must obviously intensify our search for him, without disclosing why we want him found and brought in. And what about this call yesterday to Sir Arnold Swallow, was that Farmer?'

'I think it must have been,' Wilcox said. 'We've checked that he's not in the habit of receiving anonymous telephone calls at his home and it's just too much of a coincidence for this one to have come out of the blue.'

'I suppose it could have been made with the idea of giving him the frighteners before Tuesday's contact is made.'

Nick nodded keenly, this having been Clare's theory.

'You agree, I gather?' the D.A.C. said, looking towards him.

'One slightly curious feature has been Sir Arnold's reaction,' Wilcox said, in a puzzled tone.

'In what way?'

'He has taken the whole thing much more emotionally than I'd have expected.'

'Is that surprising?'

'I can't help feeling,' Wilcox went on, apparently groping to express himself, 'that he's been more personally affected than if this was just a demand by some outside blackmailer. That he somehow fears what the investigation may disclose. I can't put it any better than that. It's a sort of feeling I've had from the outset and which has been fortified every time I've seen Sir Arnold.'

'Do you share the feeling?' the D.A.C. asked Nick.

'Yes, sir, I think I do. It's simply that I'd have expected someone in his position, chairman of a great company and all that, to have reacted with greater detachment.'

The D.A.C. made a face indicating his own detachment from the view expressed.

'I don't know that one has to expect all business tycoons to react like efficient machines in a crisis. However, I'm the last person to knock other people's hunches. If you feel as you do, Jack, why not probe that aspect? But do it discreetly and don't waste too much time on it.'

'It shouldn't take long either to disprove my hunch or to provide it with substance,' Wilcox said, giving Nick a friendly smile. 'I wouldn't have mentioned it at all if I hadn't been aware that Nick felt something of the same sort.'

'All right, that's settled,' the D.A.C. said. 'Now I want

to run over our plans once the blackmailer makes contact. They're bound to be contingent at this stage, but we need to discuss them as far as we can. After all, once he does make contact, it's unlikely we shall have time for leisurely conferences. The pressure'll be on, that's for sure . . .'

When the meeting broke up, it was made clear to Nick that Wilcox was his guvnor for the day. As the two of them walked down one of the Yard's endless corridors, Wilcox said, 'I think we might put our hunch to the test right away.'

Nick was quick to note that it was 'our' hunch and wondered whether he ought to be flattered or whether it was said in order to ensure he would take his share of any criticism that might subsequently be going.

'We'll check with C.R.O.,' Wilcox went on, 'to find out if they have any files under the name of Swallow. It's just possible they might come up with something interesting.'

Twenty minutes later, they were examining the file of one Rupert Armitage Swallow, aged 30, who had five previous convictions. Three of them were for passing dud cheques and two for motoring offences. At the age of 19 he had been placed on probation for taking and driving away a car without the owner's consent and two years later he had been fined and had been disqualified from driving after being convicted of causing a death by dangerous driving.

'The next thing to find out,' Wilcox said, 'is whether he's any relation to the Swallows of Swallow Sugar. Is Sir Arnold's middle name Armitage by any chance?'

'I don't think so, sir. But it could be his mother's maiden name.'

'We could find that out easily enough.'

'Or better still, sir, why don't we speak to the officer in charge of his last case? He got two years imprisonment, which means that he won't have been out many months.'

It didn't take very long to discover that the officer's name was Detective Sergeant Tait and that he was currently serving on C Division.

Nick put through a call and a few moments later was speaking to Tait, to whom he explained that he was working on an enquiry with Detective Chief Superintendent Wilcox.

'The name of Swallow has cropped up,' he said, 'and I see that you were concerned with a bloke of that name a couple of years ago.'

'Is he in trouble again?' Sergeant Tait said cheerfully. 'I'm not surprised, mind you. Nasty bit of work. He ought to have got more than two years, but he came up in front of one of those judges who sees good in everyone. And, of course, his name helped.'

'His name?' Nick said, with a sudden prickle of excitement.

'He's the son of Sir Whatnot Swallow, the chairman of Swallow Sugar, not that his old man came forward on his behalf. I gather he cut him out of his life several years ago. He's a real bad seed, the son. Incidentally, he's the offspring of an early marriage which didn't last. The first Lady Swallow, or rather Mrs Swallow at that time, decamped when the boy was only a few years old. Went off to South Africa with a diamond millionaire, I was told. I got all this information when I was preparing his antecedents for the Court. Anyway, what's Master Swallow done this time?'

'He mayn't have done anything. His name happened to come up on our screen and Mr Wilcox wanted him checked on.'

'He'll be in trouble again before long, if he isn't already,' Tait remarked in the same cheerful tone. 'But I don't think there's much else I can tell you about him. I've not had anything to do with him since he got time in my case.'

'Did you have any contact with his father?'

'No. That is, unless you call a terse letter from the old man's solicitors saying he didn't want to know about it contact.'

'Did the son ever talk to you about his father?'

'Not as I recall. I think each had given the other up as a bad job.'

'What exactly had the son done in your case?'

'Dropped dud cheques round a number of West End stores. Clothes and booze for the most part.'

'From which I assume he was short of money?'

'Like me! Except I don't go around ordering cases of brandy and champagne and buying half a dozen pairs of silk pyjamas at a time in Jermyn Street.'

'Well, thanks for all the information,' Nick said. 'I'm glad I called you.'

'A pleasure. If you happen to run into him, don't bother to give him my regards.'

Wilcox, who had listened to the conversation on an extension, hung up and gave Nick a pleased look.

'So Sir Arnold has a ne'er-do-well son with expensive tastes and no money!'

'And who came out of prison only a short time ago,' Nick added.

'All of which could account for Sir Arnold Swallow's reaction to the blackmail letter. Though not ready to admit anything to us, he fears that his own son could be behind it.' He looked thoughtful for a moment. 'It seems, Nick, as though our hunch may have some substance after all.'

'If it is Rupert Swallow, sir, we've still to find out how he came to use Sipson's code in his letter.'

Wilcox peered at Nick over the top of his spectacles. 'I think you must get used to the idea that you may have arrested the wrong man. However, first things first, we must obviously find Swallow and ask him some pertinent questions. After which, we shall either be able to eliminate him from the enquiry or we shall have added another suspect to our list.'

CHAPTER TEN

Minnie Dove came through the door that separated the private part of the premises from the public and gave the saloon bar a swift, appraising look.

It was empty even for a Monday evening; not that any evening of the week, apart from Saturdays, ever saw it more than a third full.

It was mad to have built a public house there in the first place and, as she had had all too much time to realise, even madder on her part to have taken it over. No-one could have run it at a profit and breaking even was difficult enough.

She picked up a glass and drew a small Scotch for herself. She poured in a fair amount of water and was about to return to her own quarters when the street door opened and a man she knew as Nat entered.

'Hello and how is Mrs Dove this evening?' he asked in an aggressively jovial tone as he approached the bar.

'Could be worse,' she replied in the first cliché that came to mind.

She had never cared for Nat anyway, but had liked him even less after being told on good authority that he was a police informant. His speciality was to haunt the pubs of the area, keep his ears open, wheedle out any interesting tid-bits of information and pass it on to the police for payment in a small way.

She was thankful that he did not appear in *The Three Ducks* very regularly, even if the obvious reason was the absence of custom.

'A bit quiet this evening, isn't it?' he remarked, glancing

about him. He turned back and gave Minnie Dove an in-gratiating smile. 'Do I have the honour of being served by the good lady herself?'

'What's your order?'

'A pint of your best. And what about a little something for yourself?'

So he was after something. He'd never have offered her a drink otherwise. Minnie decided to wait and find out what he wanted.

'Thank you. I'll have a small Scotch,' she said demurely, pouring it into the glass she already held.

'Cheers, Mrs Dove.'

'Cheers.'

'Don't see many of the familiar faces this evening,' he observed, once more glancing round the saloon bar. 'Which reminds me, what's happened to that chap who was always on about having got the sack from his firm.'

'I wonder which chap you mean,' she replied, in an innocent voice.

'You must remember! Chap with a long mournful face. What was his name?'

'Do you mean Mr Farmer?'

He gave the counter a resounding slap. 'That's the chap,' he said eagerly. 'Haven't seen him around for a while.'

'He's gone away.'

'Gone away! Where's he gone to?'

'I can't tell you. He just went sudden-like.'

'He'll be in touch with you before long, I'll be bound.'

'What makes you say that?'

'A little bird did tell me that he was more than a little fond of you, Mrs Dove,' he said coyly.

'It's the first I've heard of it.'

'The same little bird went even further and suggested you and he might be contemplating matrimony.'

'What, me and Mr Farmer? I've never heard such nonsense,' she remarked with a good-natured laugh.

Nat laughed, too. 'One hears so many things. Anyway, I'm

sure it's not for lack of opportunity that you've never re-married. You're an attractive woman, Mrs Dove.'

'And you're just a flatterer, who listens to too many little birds,' she replied.

He leaned confidentially across the bar and in a hoarse whisper said, 'You know you can trust me, the truth is I was told you had recently re-married.'

Minnie Dove drew back and glared at him. 'Now who told you that?'

'It was just a rumour I happened to pick up,' he said defensively.

'Where did you pick it up? Who've you been discussing my private life with? I want to know, so that I can put an end to rumours of that sort. Come on, tell me!'

Her tone was such that Nat retreated a step. 'I haven't been discussing your private life with anyone,' he protested.

'Then where'd you hear this rumour?'

He licked his lips nervously. 'I haven't heard it actually.'

'Then what do you mean?'

'I just wanted ... I just wondered if you and Mr Farmer *had* got married. So I thought I'd pretend that I'd heard you had. I'm sorry, I didn't mean to upset you.'

Minnie Dove stuck out her chin and said aggressively, 'And what's it to you even if Mr Farmer and I had got married? What business of yours would it be, may I ask?'

'You've got me all wrong, Mrs Dove,' he said in a placating tone. 'I was only enquiring as a friend.'

Minnie Dove stared at him for a while as a small spider might observe the futile throes of a trapped bluebottle. Then she said, 'I think it'd be best if you finished your drink and left. And I'd be glad if in future you would do your drinking on someone else's premises, because you certainly won't be welcome here.'

Nat gave a shrug and swallowed the remainder of his beer.

'I'm sorry you've taken it this way,' he said on a note of false dignity.

After he had gone, Mrs Dove sought out the young barman

who at that moment was serving in the public bar.

'I'm going upstairs to my room, Paul,' she said. 'And by the way, I shall be out most of tomorrow.'

'That's O.K., Mrs Dove.'

'But I'll be back by opening time in the evening.'

'Don't you worry, Mrs Dove, I'll look after everything.'

'If anyone wants me, just say I've gone out.'

CHAPTER ELEVEN

When Herbert's trial resumed on the Tuesday morning, the court-room was packed. This was largely accounted for by the influx of press men whose ever-sensitive antennae had told them something was up. News had quickly got round of the judge's unusual adjournment into chambers on Friday afternoon and of his not sitting on the Monday.

One enterprising reporter had gone so far as to keep an eye on the block of flats in Kensington where Mr Justice Tidyman lived. His reward had been to observe the judge make a sortie to a nearby supermarket in the morning and to take a small and ancient dog for a walk in Kensington Gardens in the afternoon. Both harmless activities in themselves, but of significance in the circumstances. Certainly neither appeared of sufficient importance to warrant the adjournment of The Queen against Herbert Sipson.

As Philip Vane glanced at them across the Court, he was reminded of a line of starlings perched along a telephone wire. There was the same air of eager expectancy.

On his own way into Court, he had been waylaid by a group of them who had assailed him with questions, from which it was clear that none had an inkling of what had happened. The most popular theory was that the judge had wished to give Herbert extra time to prepare his defence in the hope he would even yet agree to be represented by counsel.

Herbert was waiting half-way up the stairs leading from the cells beneath the court-room to the dock when he heard the knocks on the door heralding the judge's entry.

The prison officer in charge of him always held him there,

out of sight of those in Court but ready for his own immediate appearance. The officer in question still remembered the roasting he had received as a young man when the judge had said, 'Put up the prisoner,' and there had been what seemed a wait of hours before anything happened, apart from the clanging of cell doors, the flushing of a distant cistern and some raucous shouts. It was a consequence of this unhappy recollection that caused Herbert to be treated like a greyhound in its starting trap.

Everyone stood as Mr Justice Tidyman entered and waited for him to go through the ritual exchange of bows with court officials and counsel before resuming their seats in a down-surge of shuffles and protesting wood.

Herbert's arrival in the dock was preceded by a prod in the ribs from the prison officer behind him on the stairs. Although the bowing ritual was over by the time he made his entrance, he didn't allow this to deter him from making his own bows to judge and jury and, finally, to prosecuting counsel.

Detective Chief Superintendent Lapham watched with an air of cynical detachment. Herbert's bows were so obsequious, he almost expected them to be accompanied by a small flurry of pidgin Japanese.

The starlings on the press benches were for their part waiting only for the judge to satisfy their curiosity and their nervous stirring was stilled as Mr Justice Tidyman began speaking.

'It is a broad principle that the courts in this country must administer justice in public.' As he uttered the word 'public', the reporters glanced at one another in disbelief at what seemed about to follow. Surely the Court was not going to sit in camera. That only happened in spy cases in their experience and yet what else was the judge leading up to? 'That principle is subject to exceptions,' Mr Justice Tidyman went on. 'The exceptions are themselves the outcome of a yet more funda-mental principle, namely that the chief objects of courts of justice must be to secure that justice is done. As the paramount object must always be to do justice, the general rule as to publicity, which, after all, is only a means to an end, must accordingly yield.' He paused and looked around the assembled court-room. 'After the most careful and anxious consideration, I have come to the conclusion that circumstances have arisen in this trial which make it necessary in the interests of justice and for public safety for the Court to sit in camera from now on. This means that press and public will be excluded.' Glancing at the dumbfounded press bench, he went on, 'I appreciate that this is a highly unusual course to take, but so are the circumstances which have dictated it. I think I have made it clear that it is not a step which has been lightly taken but I am satisfied that it is necessary both in the interests of justice to this accused and in the public interest.' He looked across at the court inspector. 'The Court will now be cleared. Only court officials, counsel and, of course, the jury may remain.'

A bewildered and indignant throng of reporters gathered outside the court-room.

'What the hell did he mean about public safety?' asked one.

'Wonder if they've connected Sipson with the I.R.A?' speculated another.

As bewilderment and indignation yielded to more militant feelings, one or two of them decided to get through to their head offices and urge that the judge's ruling should be tested by an immediate application to a higher court for some writ or another – no-one was very sure which writ if any would do the trick.

'I'm not certain we don't have more to write about as it is,' one of them remarked. 'Secret justice, dangerous precedents and all that.'

'Bugger that!' one of the others exclaimed angrily. 'I want to know what's going on in that trial and somehow I'm going to find out.'

Their deliberations were broken by the expulsion of a final member of the public and by an irrevocable click as the door of the Court was locked behind them.

Herbert, who had been taken as much by surprise as the

newspaper men, sat waiting for the judge's next move with a slightly anxious air. He knew that he must be more attentive then ever and fearlessly ready to intervene if the judge was about to take unfair advantage of him. So long as the press was present, judges were more or less obliged to mind their ps and qs, but, without such an inhibiting influence, Herbert had little faith in their much vaunted impartiality. In particular, he had not the slightest doubt that Mr Justice Tidyman would pot him if he could. That was confirmed by the fact that he was letting the trial continue after it had become obvious that Herbert must be innocent.

The court inspector indicated that the judge's directions had been executed and Mr Justice Tidyman turned towards the jury, who were sitting with the air of patients in a dentist's waiting-room.

'You will have been wondering, members of the jury, what this is all about and I will now explain it to you. Last Friday, the prosecution came into possession of a document which could be seen as most relevant to the defence. In accordance with normal practice and with the principle of fairness which obtains in our Courts, the document in question has been made available to the accused. It is, of course, up to him what use he makes of it and therefore it is not for me at this stage to tell you of its contents. The time for that will come later. Suffice it to say that the document is one, disclosure of which, other than in circumstances of privacy, would, in my judgment be inimical to the public interest. It remains only to say this, members of the jury, the proceedings which take place while the Court is sitting in camera must not be disclosed outside these walls. And now, Mr Vane,' he went on, turning in the direction of prosecuting counsel, 'please call your next witness.'

Before Philip Vane could rise to his feet, however, Herbert had jumped up.

'I should like to read the letter to the jury, my lord,' he said excitedly, waving the piece of paper in front of him.

'Not now,' the judge interrupted.

'But, my lord ...'

'I said, not now. You will have an opportunity to introduce it into evidence at a later stage.'

'But they ought to know now ...'

'Kindly don't argue with me.'

Herbert's shoulders drooped as he cast the jury an anguished look. One or two jurors returned him glances of surreptitious sympathy, which Herbert noted with quiet satisfaction and the judge with a stony expression.

'I'll call Detective Chief Superintendent Lapham, my lord,' Vane announced.

Lapham rose from his seat at the table in the well of the Court and took the few paces to the witness box.

His evidence-in-chief consisted largely of describing his interviews with Herbert after his arrest.

He was an experienced witness who had over the years faced cross-examination of every sort. He was used to pitting his wits against wily and even dishonest advocates, as well as those whose very charm and courtesy was all part of a guileful plan. He was as wary of the friendly approach as he was armoured against hostility. His defects were those most commonly seen in police witnesses, an inability ever to admit an error and a tendency to sound self-righteous when repudiating suggestions of improper conduct, both being attributes bred by the system.

When Vane sat down, Lapham half-turned in the direction of the dock to meet Herbert's first question. His expression was one of massive imperturbability.

'I want to question the witness about this letter,' Herbert said in an implacable tone.

'Very well,' the judge replied.

Herbert seemed taken by surprise by Mr Justice Tidyman's obliging response.

Quickly recovering himself, however, he went on, 'I should like the jury to have copies of it in front of them, my lord, but unfortunately I don't have the same facilities as the prosecution for copying documents.' He gave the Court a pleased smile.

'There's no need to be facetious,' the judge remarked. He turned towards Vane. 'Are there copies available?'

'No, my lord. I thought it unwise, having regard to the circumstances of the letter, to have it copied indiscriminately.'

Mr Justice Tidyman nodded. 'I commend your judgment. Well, you've heard, Mr Sipson, there aren't copies, but you may hand the one you have to the witness and get him to identify it.'

The usher reached up and accepted the document from Herbert as though it was about to burst into flames. He handed it to Lapham who, for his part, gave it a cursory glance as it might have been yesterday's newspaper.

'Is that an exact copy of a letter sent to the Swallow Sugar Company?' Herbert asked eagerly.

'It's a photostat copy,' the judge broke in. 'There's no need to ask if it's an exact copy.'

'Well, go on, answer,' Herbert said.

'I have no first-hand knowledge to enable me to answer,' Lapham replied in a primly defiant tone. Swinging round to face the judge, he went on, 'My lord, the only information I have concerning this letter is hearsay.'

Mr Justice Tidyman didn't look up from his notebook for a few moments. When he did, his expression might have been that of Saint Sebastian on being pierced by yet another arrow.

'Within limits the Court will accept that position.'

'It's no good handing me this document if I'm then going to be frustrated using it,' Herbert expostulated.

'Kindly be quiet,' the judge commanded. He turned back to Lapham who was glowering in the witness-box. 'Is it within your knowledge that the original of the letter of which you have a copy in your hand was received through the ordinary mail last Thursday by the chairman of the Swallow Sugar Corporation?'

'I've only been told that,' Lapham said, without any attempt to disguise his anger. They just bent the rules whenever it suited them, he reflected savagely. To think of the number of times he had been rapped for giving bits of hearsay evidence. Bloody hypocrite lawyers!

'You have no reason to doubt it, however?' the judge remarked.

'No.' Lapham's tone was bleak.

'Well, that's one hurdle surmounted,' Mr Justice Tidyman murmured. 'Yes, continue your questions, Mr Sipson.'

'Will you read the letter out to the jury please?' Herbert said.

Lapham glanced towards the judge who gave him a nod. Now, there are wide varieties of expression that can go into the reading aloud of any documents. Suffice it to say that Lapham did his best to make the letter in question sound as irrelevant as a circular sent to city dwellers announcing a small increase in the price of farm fertiliser. All his efforts failed, however, to blunt the manifestly intense interest of the jury.

When he finished, he put the letter on the ledge in front of him with the air of a man who has just completed a particularly tedious chore.

'Has that letter been written by the same person who wrote the one to Shangri-La Bingo?'

'I have no idea who *wrote* this letter,' Lapham replied, disdainfully.

'But anyone can see it must have been written by the same person,' Herbert exclaimed.

'Whether it was or not is essentially a matter for the jury to decide,' the judge broke in. 'Let them see the copy.'

While they were reading it in groups of three or four with expressions of avid interest, Herbert watched them with an air of benign care while Lapham stood in the box giving an imitation of bored detachment.

When the jury had finished, the letter was passed up to the judge who said, 'Before we go any further, there are one or two observations I wish to make about this document.' He gave the jury a look which commanded their attention. 'Members of the jury, I think it will now be apparent to you why I judged it necessary for the court to sit in camera. The letter which you have just read was, as you have heard, received last Thursday by the chairman of the Swallow Sugar Corporation. The postmark on the envelope showed that it had been posted in London the previous day, that is to say the day before this trial began. It is not for me at this stage to express any view as to the authorship of the letter nor as to any suggested similarities between it and the letter which was sent to the Shangri-La Bingo Company in this case. And, indeed, it is not on account of either of those matters that we are sitting in camera. In the first place, as you will realise, the police are conducting an intensive, though necessarily clandestine, investigation of this further letter and in the second – and this is the real reason for my decision – it would clearly excite a great deal of public alarm if details of the threat contained in the letter were to become known. Every possible step is being taken by the authorities involved to ensure that such details are not publicly disclosed, at least until the threat itself has been neutralised. I cannot therefore impress upon you too strongly, members of the jury, that you should not breathe one word about the matter outside this Court.' He glanced along the two rows of jurors as though seeking an indication of their understanding of the position. A number did, in fact, give small nods of assent. He turned his gaze in Herbert's direction. 'Yes and now I suppose you wish to continue your cross-examination?'

Herbert gave the judge a bow and switched his attention back to Lapham.

'Have type-writing tests been conducted on this new letter?'

'I don't understand your question.'

'Have the police tried to discover whether both letters were typed on the same machine?'

'The original of this letter has been handed to the laboratory for examination, if that answers your question.'

'And what's the answer?'

'I can't tell you.'

'Why not?'

'Because I've not made the examination myself.'

The judge once more groaned inwardly. 'Have you seen a laboratory report yet, Mr Vane?' he asked.

'No, my lord.'

'Well, perhaps you would ascertain the position and let the Court know.'

Vane nodded and Mr Justice Tidyman addressed Herbert. 'Once a report is available you will be supplied with a copy.'

'Thank you, my lord. I am grateful for your lordship's kind indulgence.'

The judge swallowed his rising bile and said, 'Get on with your questions, if you have any more.'

'Do you agree that there are many similarities between the two letters?'

Lapham appeared to weigh the question carefully before vouchsafing a reply.

'That's a matter of opinion,' he said finally.

'And what is your opinion?'

'Is my opinion relevant, my lord?' he enquired in a faintly contemptuous tone.

'No, it is not,' Mr Justice Tidyman replied, rapidly reaching the conclusion that he was as fed-up with Lapham's pig-headedness as with Herbert's phony obsequiousness. 'The issue of similarity between the two letters is one for the jury and you will have an opportunity of addressing them on it in due course,' he said to Herbert. 'I suggest you leave the topic so far as this witness is concerned and move on to another.'

Herbert frowned. Instead of ordering him to lay off, the judge should be making Lapham answer his questions. The chief superintendent was being obstinate and unfair and was being allowed to get away with it. It was monstrous that his trial was continuing, anyway. The whole system was weighted against him. It just was not fair. He realised that the jury was looking at him and he quickly gave them one of his small sad smiles.

'Do you have any further questions to ask the witness?' the judge enquired.

Herbert swallowed in the manner of a child overcoming its grief and assumed a sorry expression as he faced Lapham once more.

'Why don't you just admit that you're convinced I'm guilty and that nothing would ever get you to change your mind? Why not be honest and admit that?'

Lapham glanced at the judge who must surely defend him against rolled-up questions of that sort. Or was Sipson licensed to ignore all the normal rules?

Wearily Mr Justice Tidyman said, 'The suggestion is that you are wholly prejudiced against the accused. Perhaps for the sake of the record we could have your answer?'

'I am not, my lord,' Lapham replied in the tone of one swearing an oath of allegiance.

'Didn't you try and make me confess?' Herbert went on.

'I most certainly did not.'

'By threats and promises?'

'No.'

'I suggest you did?'

'I didn't.'

'Well, if he did, he appears to have been quite unsuccessful,' the judge commented.

'I never did, my lord,' Lapham said indignantly.

'But he tried, my lord. He knows he did.'

'Yes, all right,' the judge said in the same weary tone. 'You can give the jury your version of events if and when you choose to give evidence on your own behalf. But as you have not made any oral admissions from which guilt might be inferred, there seems no point in cross-examining this witness to the effect that he used improper means to induce you to confess.'

'If you say so, my lord.'

'I do.'

'Then that completes my cross-examination,' Herbert announced, bowing first to the judge and then to the jury before resuming his seat.

At this point there was a flurry of whispering at one end of the jury box and an embarrassed male juror stood up and asked in an urgent voice if he might go to the lavatory.

'The Court will adjourn for ten minutes,' Mr Justice Tidyman declared, not without apparent relief.

As he emerged into the corridor, Lapham was set upon by a couple of reporters who were maintaining a vigil outside the court-room.

'What's this in aid of?'

'You know I can't tell you a thing,' Lapham replied, lighting a cigarette.

'Not even off the record?'

'Not even that.' He grinned at them. 'You're wasting your time.'

'Give us a clue. We might be able to help.'

'Help me get put inside for contempt of court most likely.'

'What's this adjournment for? What's come up now? Can you tell us that?'

'A juror's been taken short.' He paused. 'There's a headline for you.'

While he had been talking, Lapham had noticed a discarded *Evening Standard* on a bench on the far side of the corridor. He now strolled across and picked it up. It was one of the early editions and he turned to the page of personal ads.

There, half-way down the column, appeared 'Swallow has ears'.

He dropped the paper back on the bench, stubbed out his cigarette and returned to Court.

If anything was going to happen, it must happen soon.

CHAPTER TWELVE

Much the same thought was passing through Sir Arnold Swallow's mind as he stared at the brief, enigmatic message.

Though the police had assured him that the paper would run it in every edition throughout the day, he had to see it with his own eyes at the earliest opportunity. Thus his secretary, Miss Gunn, had been sent out to buy a paper from the newsvendor along the street.

It was while he was just staring at it that Ralph Swallow came into the room, a copy of the *Evening Standard* in his hand.

'Oh, you've already got one, I see.'

'Yes, Miss Gunn went out for it.'

'All we can do now is wait. The longer we go without a response, the more likely the whole thing was a loathsome hoax.'

'The police think we shall hear within twenty-four hours; forty-eight at the most.'

'That's on the basis that it's genuine blackmail.'

'I take it there's still no trace of Farmer.'

Ralph Swallow shook his head. 'I'm sure we'd have heard if they'd found him.'

'It seems curious that he vanished at just that particular time ...' Sir Arnold's voice trailed away.

'It doesn't strike me as curious at all. It merely confirms one's suspicions that he's the man.'

'It'll certainly be a relief to know that,' Sir Arnold remarked in an almost wistful tone. Then turning his head slowly, he looked straight into his cousin's eyes and said, 'I'm so worried it might be someone else. I have been all along.'

For a second Ralph Swallow appeared mystified. 'Rupert?' he asked in a doubtful tone.

Sir Arnold nodded. 'Yes, Rupert.'

'Have you heard from him recently?'

'He's been in touch with me once since his release from prison. He wanted money.'

'And?'

'I refused.'

'But you've no reason to think he's behind this blackmail?'

'Put like that, I've no reason not to,' Sir Arnold remarked bleakly. 'He ... he has shown himself to be a person without scruple.' The next words came in a rush. 'He's a criminal, Ralph. A criminal with a criminal mind. And if he's not our blackmailer, I can only say that he'd be capable of being so.'

There was a pause during which both men stared into space.

'Do you know where he's living?' Ralph Swallow asked at length.

Sir Arnold shook his head. 'I gathered he was in London, but he never gave me his address.' He paused and added, 'I didn't want to know it and there was no point, anyway.'

'I still wouldn't think this was in keeping with Rupert's record,' Ralph Swallow said in a reassuring tone. 'I mean, he may have come to you for money, but has he ever shown any spite when you've refused him?'

'No-o, he's never threatened to get his own back or anything of that sort, but that isn't the same as saying he wouldn't contemplate action against me. You remember that burglary I had just before he went to prison. A lot of old silver was taken. I couldn't help wondering then whether he wasn't the person responsible. I don't mean that he was the actual burglar, but I still wonder whether he didn't put one of his crooked friends up to it.'

'But wasn't it one of a number of burglaries in your area at the time?'

'Yes, but I still couldn't help wondering.' He paused. 'What's worrying me is that I've not told the police about Rupert. I ought to have done so. It's for them to eliminate him from the enquiry if they can. And certainly no-one could be more relieved than I if they do. But I've never even mentioned his name to them ...'

'If it'll make you feel happier,' Ralph Swallow said, 'I'll give Chief Superintendent Wilcox a ring and explain the situation to him.'

'Thank you, Ralph, but it's plainly something I should do myself. I'll be thankful to get it off my chest. It has helped discussing it with you. I've been weighed down by worry these past few days.' He gave a shiver. 'Not that there still isn't enough to worry about, Rupert apart.'

Rupert Armitage – he had dropped the name of Swallow after coming out of prison – gazed at the sulky girl sitting on the edge of the bed and pouting her displeasure with life.

'Stop wingeing, kitten, I keep on telling you that everything's going to be all right soon.'

'I know you keep on saying that, but nothing ever happens,' the girl replied.

'It will soon.'

'I'm fed up with this grotty little room,' she went on, gazing about her with distaste.

'We'll soon have somewhere much better.'

'Where?'

'We'll go abroad if you like. It mightn't be a bad idea, anyway.'

'I've always wanted to go to Florida,' she said. 'All those beaches and they have wonderful night-clubs too.'

'O.K., Florida it shall be!'

'But when?'

'Quite soon. Just be patient for a little bit longer.'

The girl's face which had temporarily lit up now assumed its sulky expression once more.

'There you go again. Promises, that's all you give me.'

'If you're not careful, I'll give you something else right now.'

She looked up at him sharply. Though he was grinning at her, there was something in his expression that frightened her. It was always there and it both frightened and excited her.

'I'm not in the mood,' she said primly.

'I'll soon make you in the mood,' he replied, taking a step towards the bed, his grin becoming closer to a leer.

Afterwards as they lay together on the bed, she said in a wheedling tone, 'You never tell me anything about yourself.'

'You know all you need to know. That I'm fun to be with, good in bed and shortly going to give you the greatest time you've ever had in Miami.'

'Is that in Florida?'

'Yes.'

'I've always wanted to go there,' she said, dreamily.

'So you said. That's why we're going. Remember?'

'But when?'

'Soon. Soon, my kitten.' He glanced at his wristwatch and got up abruptly. 'And now I've got to go out for a couple of hours.' He held up an admonitory hand as she seemed about to speak. 'And don't ask me why or where. Just trust me for a little bit longer.' He bent down and kissed her. 'There's a good kitten,' he said in the tone that always held a faint note of menace. 'Wait till I come back and I'll take you out this evening. That's a promise.'

'Have you got your key with you, Mr Butler?' the voice called out.

Farmer gave a small start. He wasn't used to being addressed by his new name. Indeed, if the question had not been so obviously directed at him, he would have closed the front door behind him without pausing.

As it was, he turned back to find Mrs Oller standing in the kitchen doorway.

'Yes, I have it,' he replied, reflecting that landladies seemed to nurse obsessions about keys.

'Good. I don't like having to answer the door unnecessarily. It's as bad as when the children were always knocking to be let in and my legs are not as young as they were in those days.'

'No, I haven't forgotten it,' he said, and quickly closed the door behind him.

He had spent most of the previous day after arriving from Reading looking for somewhere to stay. It had not been easy to find anywhere within his price range, but around tea-time when he was thoroughly footsore he had come across Mrs Oller's small terraced house not far from the prison.

His room was not as agreeable as the one he'd had at Reading, but he consoled himself with the thought that he probably would not be staying there long, even though he had again had to pay a week's rent in advance.

A short walk brought him to the main post office and he made a bee-line for a telephone kiosk.

The bell at the other end seemed to ring endlessly before it was answered and then by an unexpected voice.

'Hello.' The voice sounded impatient.

'Is that *The Three Ducks*?'

'Yes.'

'I'd like to speak to Mrs Dove.'

'She's out.'

'Out?' Farmer's tone was one of surprise.

'She won't be back till this evening. Who's that speaking?'

'Mr Farmer.'

'Oh, I didn't recognise your voice. This is Paul.'

'Oh, hello.' Farmer's surprise turned to diffidence. He hadn't addressed more than half a dozen words to Paul in his life. 'She didn't mention she was going to be out today. I spoke to her yesterday evening.'

'She didn't tell me until closing time. I imagine it was something she decided on the spur of the moment. Anyway, I must get back into the bar. Any messages?'

'No.'

Leaving the telephone kiosk he walked over to a counter and purchased two letter cards.

From the post office, he made his way to a café in the High, buying a copy of the *Evening Standard* on his way. While his cup of tea cooled, he read the paper from cover to cover, apparently giving equal attention to each page, regardless of content.

Tucking the paper under his arm, he walked briskly back to his lodging. He got into the house and up to his room without evoking Mrs Oller's interest.

Once in his room, he locked the door and got out his typewriter.

Clare finished her frugal lunch of a poached egg and the remainder of some stewed figs and sat down in an armchair with a large cup of coffee which she reckoned to be the best part of the meal.

Apart from her vast size, she felt surprisingly well and at general peace with the world. She had no regrets at having given up her career on marriage. Though she had enjoyed her time in the police, she had regarded it more as an interlude in her life than as a permanent career. About one thing she had not the slightest doubt, namely that, having been a police officer, she was much better equipped than most to be the wife of one. Her understanding of all the unpredictable calls liable to be made on Nick's time would prevent her fussing – and, worse still, carping.

As she sat luxuriously sipping her coffee, she thought about his present case. And that was really the fundamental issue, she reflected, was it case or cases? Were the two blackmail demands separate and independent? Or did they form part of a single scheme?

It was not enough to say that there were too many coincidences for them to be necessarily one transaction. Anyone who had served in the police knew that almost every major enquiry of any complexity threw up remarkable coincidences and that hours of valuable time were wasted pursuing red herrings of a monstrously fortuitous variety.

On the other hand, the letters sent to the Shangri-La Bingo Company and to the Swallow Sugar Corporation could not possibly be described as coincidences. Either they had been conceived in the same brain or the person who had sent the second letter had deliberately set about giving that impression. Which meant that the sender of the second letter knew all about the first.

If Herbert Sipson was the sender of the first letter, then it must be someone who knew all about it who had made the demand on Swallow Sugar. But supposing Sipson was wholly innocent – and, after all, the evidence against him was not without deficiencies – what then? And where did Farmer and now this errant son of Sir Arnold Swallow fit in? Clare felt somehow sure that Farmer did fit in, even if unable to say how. On the other hand she was inclined to write off Rupert Swallow as a red herring.

She was finding difficulty in keeping her eyes open and reached out to put down her cup before she dropped it.

She struggled to stay awake as she tried to analyse the significance of one particular coincidence. It was the only real coincidence in the whole affair. But sleep overcame her before she could do more than decide to reflect upon it urgently later.

It was the receipt of the Swallow Sugar letter on the very day that Herbert Sipson's trial opened.

The two events swam mistily around her mind as she nodded off.

CHAPTER THIRTEEN

By seven o'clock on Wednesday morning, Sir Arnold Swallow was finishing his breakfast and preparing to leave for London.

He tried to conceal from his wife the tension he felt – as also from the pretty young woman police officer whom Wilcox had installed the previous day to monitor telephone calls to the house.

It was only with difficulty that Sir Arnold had been dissuaded from sleeping in his office.

Now as he opened the front door and took his first breath of fresh air that day, he found himself staring at the Rolls, with Mason standing by the open rear passenger door, as though it were a hearse waiting to take him on his final journey.

The whole of the previous afternoon had been a torment as he waited for Mr X to get in touch. He had half-expected that as soon as their reply appeared in the paper, Mr X would be on the telephone with instructions. But it wasn't so.

Today, however, something had to happen. This was the police view, too.

He arrived at Swallow House just before eight o'clock. Miss Gunn was already in her office and jumped up with a nervous air as he entered.

'Good morning, Sir Arnold,' she said in a breathless voice.

'Good morning. Is my mail up yet?' he asked, passing through her office to his own.

'I phoned down a few minutes ago, Sir Arnold, and it hadn't arrived, but I'll go down and wait if you wish.'

'Better not. It might look suspicious.'

'It should be here any minute, Sir Arnold. It's always here by a quarter past eight.'

Sir Arnold Swallow went across to his desk and sat down, but almost immediately got up again. He walked over to the side table on which lay a selection of daily papers. He glanced at the headlines without taking them in.

There was a knock on his door and he swung round as though ready to shoot an intruder. Ralph Swallow and Nick Attwell came in.

'Sergeant Attwell wanted to be here when you opened your mail,' Ralph Swallow said.

'I'm expecting it any moment.'

It was the first time Nick had seen Sir Arnold since the police had discovered for themselves the details of his son's criminal activities and he found that he was looking at the chairman of Swallow Sugar with a distinctly jaundiced eye, even though he had now belatedly volunteered the information himself.

For a couple of minutes they stood in awkward silence, then the connecting door with the secretary's room opened and Miss Gunn appeared.

'Here is your personal mail, Sir Arnold,' she said, putting on his desk about half a dozen letters and an oblong package. She beat a hurried retreat as though expecting one or all immediately to explode.

'May I just look at that?' Nick said, indicating the package.

It was wrapped in brown paper, and bore a small, white label with Sir Arnold's name typed on it. It was marked, 'Personal and Strictly Private'.

Nick put it down again and picked up the letters. Glancing quickly at each in turn, he suddenly held one next to the package and examined both together.

'This letter-card and the package are both post-marked Oxford yesterday,' he said. 'Each is marked "Personal and Strictly Private" and the addresses appear to have been typed on the same machine.' He turned to Sir Arnold. 'Do you have a pair of scissors, sir?'

Sir Arnold opened a drawer in his desk and produced a pair.

Holding the letter-card delicately at one end, Nick cut round the perforated edges and opened it up without actually touching its front or back.

'We'll want to check it for fingerprints,' he said as he manoeuvred it for reading.

Sir Arnold and Ralph Swallow came round either side of him. The letter read:

'Dear Sir, I am glad to see that you have reacted sensibly. Full instructions about how to pay the money will follow shortly. So stand by and be ready for immediate action. Yours faithfully, Mr X.

P.S. Just to show you that I mean business, I am sending you separately a 2lb packet of Swallow Sugar mixed with an ounce of ground glass. I am sure you'll agree it's not very easy to detect even when you know it's there. And, of course, if you didn't happen to know ... I'm sure you get the point.

P.P.S. You'll notice that every "i" in this letter is typed in red. In my next, it'll be every "j".'

'So that's what the package contains,' Nick remarked. 'I suggest we don't open it, but pass it to the lab for examination.'

Sir Arnold nodded. 'I don't imagine the man's bluffing,' he said, stiffly.

'Oh, I'm pretty sure we shall find glass granules mixed with the sugar,' Nick replied.

'It looks as if he means business, Arnold,' Ralph Swallow observed.

'At least we've got a postmark to go on,' Nick said. 'That's something. It also means that Mr X is on the move for some reason. His previous letter was posted in London.'

It was as Nick was about to take his leave that Sir Arnold called him back.

'Do you have any news of my son?' he asked in a tight voice.

'None as yet. Incidentally, does he have any connections with Oxford?'

'Not that I'm aware of. But it's not like a remote Welsh village, is it? It's a big town and only fifty miles from London. I don't see that the postmark is going to help you very much.'

'Maybe not. But nine-tenths of this job is slogging routine and perseverance. Everything has to be followed up. Everything.'

Nick put a call through to Wilcox on Sir Arnold's direct outside line, so by-passing the company's own switchboard.

'You'd better bring the letter and package back here and then go down to the Old Bailey and let Mr Lapham know the latest score. I'll probably take the stuff across to the lab myself and wait while they make a preliminary examination. I've spoken to Dr Smith there and he's arranged priority facilities.'

By the time Nick reached the Court, he found that Lapham had already spoken to Wilcox on the phone and was in conference with prosecuting counsel.

'Come in, come in,' Vane called out, as Nick peered round the door of the room in which they were conferring. 'I gather things have moved, but not very far.'

'That just about sums it up, sir.'

'From what I hear, there seems little doubt that today's letter was written by the same person as the previous ones.'

'The same identifying code was used.'

'Precisely.' Vane lifted the back of his wig and scratched his head. 'We shall obviously have to inform the accused of this latest development in the same way that we told him about the other letter.'

'Just so that he can put in a lot of hearsay evidence,' Lapham said slowly. 'I thought this judge was meant to be a good one, too. All I can say is that he seems to let Sipson get away with everything.'

'Don't let's go through all that again,' Vane said with a disarming smile. 'The point is I'd better have a word with the judge before he sits and tell him what's happened.'

While Vane went off to do this, Lapham and Nick made

their way down to court where they ran into a waiting throng of newspapermen.

'What's the position this morning, Mr Lapham?' one asked.

'Same as yesterday as far as I know.'

'You mean, the Court's still sitting in camera?'

'That would be my guess.'

'What the hell's going on?' another asked in an exasperated tone.

'You'll find out one day.'

'Has this ever happened before in your experience?'

'Your paper this morning tells me it hasn't,' Lapham replied sardonically. 'Look, it's no good pestering me. You know I can't tell you anything without being in contempt of court, so lay off, will you, and let me get into the bloody Court.'

Nick noticed that one or two of the reporters exchanged quizzical looks at his use of the expletive. It was apparent to them that Lapham was out of sympathy with what was happening and that, at least, provided them with a matter of interesting speculation.

A few minutes later Mr Justice Tidyman took his seat and Herbert stepped to the front of the dock with the same bright, expectant air that marked his appearance each morning and bestowed his customary bows on judge, jury and prosecuting counsel. Nick, who was watching him, thought he detected a special gleam in his eye when he glanced into the well of the Court where the police were sitting.

Mr Justice Tidyman cleared his throat in judicial manner and said, 'I would remind everyone that the Court is still sitting in camera and is likely so to continue for the remainder of the trial. Before we proceed this morning, there is a further piece of information which has come into the possession of the prosecution and which they rightly feel should be made available to the accused. I understand that the Swallow Sugar Corporation have today received a further communication from a person signing himself as Mr X. This communication bears the red letter identification code, if I may so call it, that appeared in the letter of which you have seen a copy.' He glanced towards the jury, who were listening to him with rapt expressions. 'I understand that copies of this further letter will be available later in the morning, but that its effect is to tell the Swallow Sugar Corporation to await further instructions as to payment of the money demanded in the earlier letter.' He paused and went on with a grimace as though he had suddenly bitten off a piece of lemon peel. 'One further matter to mention in connection with this fresh communication is that it refers to a packet of Swallow Sugar sent under separate cover which has been adulterated with ground glass. Such a packet was received by the same post and is, I understand, being scientifically examined at this moment.'

'May we know why it was sent?' The question came from a long-haired young man who was one of the jurors. He was half-standing and looking towards the judge with a faintly challenging expression.

'I understand the letter refers to its despatch as an earnest of Mr X's intention if his demands are not met,' the judge replied in a tone of distaste.

'Ah!' the juror observed, sitting down again and turning to whisper to his neighbour.

Mr Justice Tidyman focused his gaze on Herbert who had assumed the quietly watchful air of a cat. The prison officer beside him motioned him to stand and he did so.

'Listen carefully to what I am about to say, Mr Sipson. The time has now come for you to present your defence. You can either go into the witness box and give evidence upon oath, in which event you will be liable to cross-examination by Mr Vane, or you can make a statement from the dock, in which case you cannot be cross-examined. I need hardly add that evidence given on oath is apt to carry greater weight than a statement not on oath, simply because it can be tested by the prosecution. But the decision is entirely yours. Now which is it to be, sworn testimony or a statement from the dock?'

'Thank you, my lord, for your patient explanation of the courses open to a defendant in this honourable Court.' Mr Justice Tidyman closed his eyes as the best way of hiding his feelings in the face of Herbert's rhetoric. Meanwhile Herbert went on, 'I am completely innocent of the charges brought against me and have nothing to fear from Mr Vane's cross-examination.' He turned and gave prosecuting counsel a small bow. 'I am quite prepared to give evidence on oath if that is what you advise, my lord.'

'I don't purport to advise,' the judge said coldly. 'You must make your own decision.'

'Well, let's make it evidence on oath then,' Herbert remarked with a chirpy look at the jury.

After he had been sworn, the judge said, 'I suggest you start by telling the jury your full name and age and occupation and go on from there. And kindly watch my pen as I shall be making a note of your evidence and I am not a shorthand writer.'

Herbert acknowledged the admonition with a bow and turned to face the jury.

'My name is Herbert Sipson and I am forty-two years old. I was born in London on the twenty-fourth of October nineteen thirty-three. I was the younger of two sons and my father was a window-cleaner.' He looked round at the judge. 'Am I going at the right speed for your lordship's pen?' he asked.

'I'll tell you when you're not,' Mr Justice Tidyman remarked tartly.

Turning back to the jury, Herbert went on in a conversational tone, 'I suppose I have to admit, good members of the jury, to having been a bit of a rolling stone in my time, though I hope you won't hold that against me. Not all of us are cast in the same mould. Not all of us lead lives of uninterrupted routine. Not all of us ...'

'You are meant to be giving evidence, not making a speech,' the judge broke in. 'What the jury want to hear is your version of events in relation to the charges brought against you.'

'I think he was about to tell them of his happy years in prison,' Vane whispered to his junior counsel. 'And that would have enabled me to cross-examine him about his previous convictions for blackmail. Pity the judge stopped him.'

'My version of events!' Herbert said in a surprised voice. 'I think you already know it, good members of the jury. I had absolutely nothing whatsoever to do with the dastardly crime I'm charged with. I did not throw a firework into the Shangri-La Bingo Hall on the evening in question or on any other evening. I did not write the letter demanding money. What's more the prosecution have completely failed to produce any evidence that I ever did either of those things. I've explained how I went to the Adonis Cinema and I, at least, good members of the jury, won't weary you with all the details again. Obviously my path crossed that of the real blackmailer that evening and in all innocence I spoilt his plan by sitting in the seat he intended to sit in. And as a result of all that, I find myself on trial at the Old Bailey after spending the past two months shut up in Brixton prison. And what do we now know, good members of the jury?' he went on in a ringing tone. 'We know that the real blackmailer is still at his evil work. At the very moment I am on trial, he is trying to get money out of the Swallow Sugar Corporation in a manner which all good citizens will condemn. Can you conceive of a more terrible threat? Let me say to you, good members of the jury, that in my view no punishment will be bad enough for that person when he is caught. And I pray, with you, good members of the jury, that he will be caught without delay.'

The judge, who had some time before laid down his pen, now broke in.

'Mr Sipson, I know it is difficult, but you keep on making a speech instead of giving evidence. You'll have an opportunity of making a speech at a later stage. Do please confine yourself to facts. Facts relevant to the issues the jury are trying.'

'I have now completed my evidence,' Herbert announced and turned to face Philip Vane with the air of a hunter facing a charging rhinoceros.

It was clear that both judge and prosecuting counsel were taken by surprise.

'He hasn't given any evidence worth the description,' Vane murmured to his junior as he rose to cross-examine.

For a few seconds he gazed at Herbert like a photographer assessing his subject's profile.

'Tell me, Mr Sipson,' he said in a tone betokening a genuine interest in the answer, 'do you usually feel beneath cinema seats?'

'Only if I drop something,' Herbert replied with a polite smile.

'As I think you probably realised, I didn't mean on the floor; I meant, do you generally feel the underside of the seat?'

'No.'

'But you did on this occasion?'

'My hand happened to touch the key as I retrieved the handkerchief.'

'That's not what the officers who were watching you say.'

'They're wrong.'

'At all events, you didn't apparently feel beneath the first seat you took?'

'I had no reason to.'

'The key was on a hook towards the back of the underside of the seat, wasn't it?'

'I'm afraid I didn't take any measurements,' Herbert replied, giving the jury a sly smile.

'Whereabouts was your fallen handkerchief?'

'Now you mention it, I seem to remember it was quite far back.'

'Is that a detail you've just invented?'

'Certainly not! That's a diabolical suggestion, Mr Vane.'

'It must have occurred to you,' Philip Vane went on imperturbably, 'that the key had been deliberately placed there?'

'I didn't give it a thought.'

'Keys can't accidentally find their way on to hooks beneath cinema seats, can they?'

'I suppose not.'

'So you must have realised it had been placed there deliberately?'

'I don't recall.'

'Try and recall.'

'I suppose I did realise it in a way, yes.'

'And yet you removed it?'

'That's right.'

'Why?'

'Why? It was the natural thing to do.'

'According to your story, it had nothing to do with you, so why not leave it where it was?'

Herbert frowned for a moment or two. 'Well, it was like finding someone's glove on the pavement. You pick it up, don't you, and put it where the owner'll find it?'

'I don't accept the analogy, but you didn't even do the equivalent of that, did you?'

'No, but I meant to. I meant to hand it in at the box office.'

'But forgot?'

'Because I was feeling unwell all of a sudden.'

'Looking back now, Mr Sipson, do you agree that your whole conduct was very odd? Very odd, that is, if you're the innocent man you profess to be?'

'No, I don't agree at all. I've been the victim of cruel circumstances, that's what I've been. Surely you must see that, too, Mr Vane?'

'I'm afraid I'm only allowed to ask questions, not answer them.'

'You'll be suggesting next,' Herbert went on, 'that I've written those letters to Swallow Sugar; that I somehow managed to type them in prison and slip out and post them.' His voice had a rising note of self-pity. 'Surely every reasonable person must see I'm innocent.'

Vane stared down at his notebook during this short outburst. He refused to give Herbert the satisfaction of his attention. If only ... if only Herbert would somehow put his character in issue so that he might cross-examine him about his previous convictions for blackmail. Victim of cruel circumstances, indeed! Admittedly it had never been a watertight case against him. There were too many gaps in the evidence, but one only had to look at Herbert to see he was a con man. And if confirmation was needed, then you only had to listen to him.

Vane glanced up as he became aware of murmurs from the other side of the Court. A number of jurors were turning and whispering to one another. Suddenly the long-haired young man among them stood up and spoke.

'Do we have to listen to any more?' he asked.

'You may stop the case in favour of the accused at any stage,' the judge replied in a tone of clear disapproval. 'On the other hand ...'

'We want to stop it now,' the young man broke in. 'We're satisfied he didn't do it.'

Herbert stood motionless, a small half-smile of triumph on his face.

At a gesture from the judge, the clerk of the court rose and addressed the jury.

'Members of the jury, are you agreed upon your verdict?'

'We are. We find Mr Sipson not guilty.'

'And is that the verdict of you all?'

'It is,' the young man declared firmly to an accompaniment of nods.

Herbert's face broke into a beaming smile as he turned towards the jury and gave them a deep bow. 'I thank you from the bottom of my heart, good members of the jury. I knew you would see that justice was done.'

'Kindly return to the dock,' the judge said.

'A travesty of justice more like,' Lapham said in an audible whisper to Nick.

When Herbert was back in the dock, Mr Justice Tidyman fixed him with a stern expression.

'Kindly listen to what I have to say to you. Any disclosure outside this Court of what has transpired since we went into camera will constitute a contempt of court and will be immediately treated as such. I cannot stress that too strongly in view of the abrupt conclusion of your trial. Do you understand?'

'I do, my lord, and may I thank your lordship for showing

me so much patience and consideration. I venture to say that today has seen British justice at its finest.'

'There's no need for further speeches now,' the judge remarked acidly. 'You are discharged.'

With a bare glance at the jury, he gave Vane a formal bow and left the Court.

The prison officer in charge tried to hurry Herbert down the cell steps to collect his belongings which had been brought to Court with him each day, but Herbert brushed him aside as he leant over the dock with arm outstretched to shake the hands of jurors filing towards the exit.

In the event they were headed off by the court usher who led them back through the bench door to avoid an encounter with any lurking newspapermen.

'I don't care a damn about the jury's verdict,' Lapham said savagely, 'we're not going to let Master Sipson out of our sight from the moment he leaves this building.'

CHAPTER FOURTEEN

About half an hour after the conclusion of the trial, Herbert was smuggled out of a side door in order that he, too, might avoid the attentions of the press. The door was closed so smartly behind him that it struck him as he paused on the threshold of freedom and propelled him into a passer-by.

Swinging his possessions in a plastic carrier-bag, he set off along the pavement.

Though he couldn't actually identify a tail, he was sure that he was under observation. It was no more than he expected.

He glanced idly about him and spotted a young man in fawn slacks and a tweed jacket and carrying a raincoat over one arm walking about fifteen yards behind him.

'That'll be him,' he murmured to himself with a small, happy smile.

A few yards on, Herbert stopped to look in the window of a cut-price tailor. The young man behind him closed about five yards and then became suddenly interested in a chemist's window.

Herbert walked back to the chemist's shop and entered, giving the young man a mild stare as he did so.

'Going to follow me in, are you?' he wondered.

But all that happened was that the young man found items of even greater interest to look at in the window.

While he negotiated the purchase of a tooth-brush which he did not want, Herbert cast continual stares out of the window to the obvious discomfiture of the young man, who eventually moved on.

When Herbert emerged from the shop, it was to see the

young man two doors on gazing with apparent absorption in the window of a launderette. He felt almost sorry for him as he turned in the opposite direction and set off at a brisk pace. Glancing over his shoulder he was not surprised to find the young man in dogged pursuit.

It made things that much simpler now he knew for sure he was being tailed. It removed the necessity of further counter-observation.

Thus satisfied he crossed the road and went into a small café where he bought a cup of tea and a strawberry jam tart. He chose a table from which he could keep on eye on the door. He saw the young man peer in and then vanish.

Herbert decided that the tea was even nastier than that served in prison and the tart was both stale and deficient in jam. Nevertheless, he took his time over his simple repast, if only because he was at liberty to do so. Liberty! What a precious commodity it was! And how undervalued by those who had never lost it!

When he had finished, Herbert carried his cup and plate back to the serving counter.

'Thanks mate,' said the large, unshaven man who was in the process of washing cups in a bowl of grey water. ''Ave a nice evening.'

'And you, too,' Herbert replied with a delighted smile. 'It's been a pleasure coming here, I assure you.'

The large man shot him a suspicious look and plunged Herbert's cup into the bowl, at the same time pointedly turning his back on the counter.

Still feeling pleased with himself, Herbert strolled out and paused on the pavement to glance left and right. There was no sign of the young man in the tweed jacket, but there was another man of about the same age standing in the doorway next to the café. He had on a pair of grey slacks and a blue blazer with silver buttons. As Herbert set off along the pavement, the young man sauntered out of the doorway and followed him.

At Chancery Lane, Herbert dived into the tube and took

a train to Oxford Circus where he changed on to the Bakerloo line and travelled to Paddington. The young man in the blue blazer did likewise.

On arrival at Paddington, Herbert walked to the Beasley Private Hotel, just off Praed Street. It was a sleazy establishment in a sleazy street, which largely catered for prostitutes and their clients, both by day and by night. The endless creakings and opening and closing of doors made sleep quite impossible for anyone who had innocently come for that purpose.

Herbert booked a room and paid for one night.

At about half past six he went out and bought an evening paper and had a light meal.

The young man in the blue blazer had been relieved, but it did not take him long to identify the replacement, not that he particularly bothered to do so. Though he was amused to note that it was a girl. He could not imagine she would be left for long keeping the Beasley under observation. She would be about as safe doing that as standing in a snake pit.

When he had finished his supper, he walked back to the hotel and went up to his room. He spread his raincoat over the grubby bedclothes and lay down, leaving the light on.

Just before midnight, in the midst of a flurry of comings and goings, he slipped out of his room and hurried along to a door marked fire exit. A few seconds later he was at the bottom of an outside escape staircase.

Moving with all the sureness of one who already knew the lie of the land, he crossed a small yard and passed through a gate into a neighbouring area and along a narrow passage which came out in the street parallel to that in which the Beasley was situated.

A quick look both ways satisfied him that there was no-one around.

A few minutes later he had boarded a late night bus.

As he tendered his fare, he felt happy and exhilarated. Excited, too.

He had had no more trouble shaking off his tail than he had

anticipated. All he'd had to do was lull them into believing he had booked in for the night.

It had all worked out as he had planned.

And that was the secret of all success. Good planning.

CHAPTER FIFTEEN

At about the same time as Herbert had been returning to the Beasley Hotel after his evening meal, Wilcox and Nick were arriving at *The Three Ducks*.

There were not more than half a dozen people in either of the two bars. The young barman named Paul hovered in a position from which he could keep an eye on both. There was no sign of Mrs Dove.

'Good evening, gentlemen,' Paul said as he moved along the bar to where they were standing, 'what's it to be?'

'A couple of pints, please,' Wilcox said, and, while the boy was drawing the beer, added, 'Mrs Dove around this evening?'

'She's upstairs. She'll probably be down later.'

'Is it possible to have a word with her?'

Paul raised his head and looked at Wilcox. 'I'll find out, if you like.'

'Please.'

'Who shall I say?'

'Just tell her it's the men from the Green Star Insurance Company who spoke to her last week.'

Paul placed their beer on the counter and took the money which Wilcox gave him. After ringing up the till, he retired to the end of the counter where a heavy red curtain covered a door and a house phone hung against the wall. It was an old-fashioned apparatus with a handle for ringing the bell at the other end.

It was answered promptly and they could hear him speaking softly without being able to distinguish the words. In due course he replaced the instrument and returned to them.

'She'll be down in about five minutes if you'll wait.'

'Thanks.'

Paul came round the end of the bar and went round the tables collecting empty mugs. It was while he was doing so that a customer rapped on the counter of the public bar and he scurried back and disappeared through the archway that joined the serving side of the two bars.

'Drink up quickly,' Wilcox said, as soon as he'd gone. 'We'll find our own way up.'

Leaving their empty glasses on the counter, they moved nonchalantly round the end of the bar and slipped through the door behind the red curtain, where they found themselves at the foot of a linoleum-covered staircase.

They tip-toed up and were about to go across to a door beneath which a light was shining when it was suddenly opened.

'What are you doing here?' Mrs Dove demanded in a hostile tone. 'I told Paul to tell you I'd be down.'

'I thought we'd save you the trouble,' Wilcox replied blandly. He looked through the door beyond her into what appeared to be some sort of sitting-room. 'Can we talk in there?'

For a few seconds it seemed as if she was going to refuse, but finally she turned back into the room and they followed her.

'Sorry to be bothering you again,' Wilcox said, 'but I'm wondering if you've had any news of Farmer?'

'I said I'd let you know when I did,' she replied.

'I know. But you're a busy woman and your priorities mayn't be the same as ours. We really are very anxious indeed to trace him.'

'I'm afraid I can't help you.'

'Can't or won't?'

She gave Wilcox a sharp look. She had never believed from the outset that they were insurance men and now she was certain they weren't. And if they weren't what they professed to be, then they must be police. And their present visit must tie up with information passed by Nat.

'I suspect that someone has been telling you stories,' she said. 'Fairy stories, at that.'

It was Wilcox's turn to look mystified. 'I'm not with you, Mrs Dove.'

'Look, Mr Insurance Man, I don't know your name because you've never told me, but I don't believe you have anything to do with the Green Star Insurance Company. I think it's much more likely that you and your young man are police officers and I also think that someone has been telling you stories, fairy stories that is, about me and Mr Farmer.' She paused and looked from Wilcox to Nick with a quizzical expression. 'So let me tell you here and now that I am not married to Mr Farmer nor do I have any intention of getting married to him, whatever your informant may have told you.'

Wilcox assumed a pained look. 'Please, Mrs Dove, you're making us sound like a couple of grubby private investigators. O.K., we're not insurance men and we are police officers, but we are desperately anxious to trace Farmer, and to trace him quickly. We came to you in the first place because we were told that he frequented your pub and we also got the impression that you'd befriended him. Indeed, you told us as much when we were here last time. But now you say you can't help us and ... well, I want to make really sure that is the case.'

As Nick listened he could not help reflecting how different Lapham's approach would have been. Altogether blunter and more brow-beating.

'All right, someone may have exaggerated your relationship with Farmer, I accept that. But it's still possible you could help us find him.'

She shook her head. 'I'm afraid that's where you're still wrong. I can't.'

She moved as though she wanted them to be gone. Indeed, Nick detected an air of unease about her which Wilcox's mollifying tone had done nothing to dissipate. From time to time she glanced nervously towards the telephone over on the sideboard, as though apprehensive of it suddenly starting to ring.

'I shall be glad if you will excuse me now as I have things I must attend to,' she said, this time moving towards the door.

For a few seconds Wilcox gazed at her dispassionately. Then giving the room a quick, appraising look, he said, 'Very well, Mrs Dove. I have no doubt, however, that we shall be in touch with you again before long. I just hope you're right about not being able to help us. You see, we have every reason to believe that Farmer may have committed a serious criminal offence and anyone who is covering up for him could also find themselves in trouble. You won't forget that, will you?'

But she hardly seemed to be listening as she ushered them out of the room. 'The door facing you at the bottom of the stairs leads out into the street,' she said hurriedly as she shut herself back inside the sitting-room.

'Obviously expecting a phone call,' Wilcox observed as they let themselves out. 'And equally obviously didn't want us to be around when it came through. I'd very much like to know why not.' He lapsed into a thoughtful silence. After a time he said, 'I wonder if we've got enough to put a case up to the Home Secretary for tapping her telephone?'

It so happened that Minnie Dove, who knew that telephones could be tapped but was unaware of all the official niceties surrounding the operation, was at that very moment deciding she must, from now on, be extremely circumspect in the use of her phone.

It was shortly after ten o'clock when Nick arrived home that evening. It had been a long, wearing and disappointing day, but as soon as he opened his front door he began to feel better. He couldn't wait to get into the living-room where he knew he would find Clare. He thought of her as unfailingly cheerful, though in anything but a hearty way; always interested to hear how the day had treated him; serene and unself-pitying. In short, he thought of her as the most desirable wife any man could have. If he had taken the trouble to analyse their relationship further, he would have realised much of her attitude flowed from the fact that she was a completely happy person at the moment.

She was watching television when he opened the door, but immediately looked up and gave him a pleased smile.

'Hungry?' she asked, after he had bent over her chair and kissed her.

'So, so.'

'Well, let's go to the kitchen and forage.'

'How are you, darling?' he asked, putting an arm round her waist.

'I'm fine.'

'And Master Attwell?' he added, as he patted her bulging front.

'Master Attwell's been very good today. Hardly had a kick out of him.'

'You don't think ...?'

'That he's sunk into a coma? No, I don't,' she said with a laugh.

In the end, Nick settled for the steak which Clare produced from the fridge.

'I thought you said we couldn't afford steak any more,' he said as she was placing it under the grill.

'There are always special occasions.'

'And what's this one?' he asked in a mystified tone.

'The great thing about special occasions is to conjure them out of thin air.'

'You mean there isn't one at all?'

'You wouldn't be having steak if there wasn't.'

'I believe you're just hoping to coax me into telling you what's happened today,' he remarked, giving her a kiss on the cheek as she was turning the steak. 'Well, listen to this for a quick run-down. Sipson has been acquitted; Mr X has written another letter; we still haven't found Farmer, though we're having Oxford taken apart stone by stone looking for him; and we still don't have a line on the black sheep son of Sir Arnold Swallow. How's that for a day of slap-downs?'

'Well, start with the first and tell me more about each.'

He had almost finished his steak by the time he had satisfied Clare's curiosity.

132

'So it looks as if Swallow Sugar will get their instructions tomorrow,' she said in a speculative tone as he concluded retailing the day's events.

'I'm not so sure. Mr X hasn't shown an inclination to move speedily so far. He may keep everyone waiting again.'

'But isn't the situation different now that Sipson is free?'

'You tell me.'

'I'm sure Herbert Sipson's release will act as a catalyst, but I can't tell you in what way.'

'You're convinced he's involved?'

She nodded. 'He must be. Though whether as a principal or as a sort of dummy stuffed in the shop window to divert attention, I just don't know.'

'One thing for certain, it can't have been he who sent the Mr X letters to Swallow Sugar. Moreover, he was as good as in self-imposed incommunicado all the time he was in Brixton prison.'

'I'm sure, Nick, that if one could only get Sipson's trial into true perspective, everything would fall into place,' Clare remarked with frowning concentration.

For a couple of minutes each of them pursued his own thoughts in silence. Then in a tone of bleak despair, Nick said, 'Here we are discussing it in the kitchen as if it were an interesting academic problem when, within a short space of time, innocent people all over the country may be writhing in agony after eating contaminated sugar. It's about the most evil, wicked and damnable crime anyone's ever perpetrated. And all we can apparently do is sit and wait for it to happen.' He looked at Clare with anguish. 'I'm not just being emotional, am I?'

'No, love,' she said, 'you're being a normal, compassionate person who, despite the disillusioning experiences of police work, still cares about his fellow humans.'

He let out a deep sigh and put out his hand. 'Let's take Master Attwell into the next room and just sit and talk about nothing special for half an hour.'

CHAPTER SIXTEEN

That same Tuesday evening the telephone rang in Sir Arnold Swallow's Berkshire home shortly after eleven o'clock.

It so happened that Sir Arnold and his wife had taken the two dogs out for their customary late night walk before locking up and retiring to bed.

In the event the phone was answered by Woman Police Constable Royston who had come on duty about an hour before.

'Is Sir Arnold Swallow there?' a male voice enquired.

'I'm afraid he's out. May I take a message?'

'Who are you?' the voice asked suspiciously.

'I'm the new maid. What do you want?'

'Tell Sir Arnold I'll call again,' the voice said and immediately rang off.

There had been something not only suspicious but also hostile about the voice and W.P.C. Royston decided to report the call immediately to her superiors at Scotland Yard.

She had hardly done so, however, when Sir Arnold and his wife and the two dogs returned to the house. She at once told him what had happened.

'There was definitely a note of menace in his tone, sir,' she said.

'You think it could have been Mr X?'

'Quite possibly, sir. When he rings again, you answer and I'll listen in on the extension. If it is Mr X, it'll be to give you instructions, sir.'

'You go on up, Marion,' he said to his wife. 'I'll just hang on down here for half an hour in case whoever it is does phone again.'

In fact, he did not have to wait longer than five minutes before the telephone began ringing. For several seconds his hand rested on the receiver while, as it seemed, he summoned up the will to lift it.

'Sir Arnold Swallow here,' he announced in a taut voice.

'I guessed you were only out with the dogs.'

W.P.C. Royston nodded to indicate that it was the same voice as before, at the same time noticing that Sir Arnold was gripping the receiver so tightly that his knuckles gleamed as though they had been polished.

'Oh, it's you! What do you want? Where are you? Yes, where are you speaking from?'

'Don't ask so many questions. But just listen.'

Placing his hand over the mouthpiece, Sir Arnold hissed at W.P.C. Royston, 'It's my son.'

'What's going on there?' Rupert enquired sharply. 'Who were you whispering to?'

'What do you want?' Sir Arnold asked.

'You know what I want. Money.'

'How much?'

'I'll let you off with a hundred and fifty thousand dollars.'

'And supposing I refuse?'

'I don't think you will this time. You won't dare.'

'How do I send you the money?'

'I want you to open an account in the name of Rupert Armitage at the Gulf Bank in Miami and pay it in dollars. You can do that easily enough through the company. In addition I want two single air tickets to Miami paid for, to await collection from British Airways at the Victoria terminal. Is that clear?'

'You have to tell me one thing,' Sir Arnold said with a note of desperation.

'What's that?'

'Are you the Mr X who sent the letters?'

For a few seconds there was no response. Then suddenly

a cackle of laughter came down the line and it went dead.

Jeffrey Farmer alias John Butler returned to his digs just before midnight. The house was in darkness and he went up to his room as quietly as possible.

He removed his jacket and shoes and loosened his tie before lying on top of the bed beneath the eiderdown.

He dozed fitfully for a while but then lay awake until the luminous dial of his watch told him it was half past five.

After dressing and combing his hair with fastidious care, he tiptoed downstairs and let himself out of the house, leaving on the hall table the note he had written. It simply said, 'Sorry, but I have been called away on urgent business. Regret any inconvenience caused. J. Butler.'

He had added the final sentence only after some reflection, deciding in the end that it might make his landlady less cross and therefore less likely to volunteer information about him should anyone start making enquiries.

He caught the first bus to Didcot and from there a train to London, a sense of caution telling him to avoid Oxford station.

It was with a feeling of relief that he merged with the anonymous crowd of early commuters at Paddington.

Leaving the platform, he made his way to a telephone kiosk.

CHAPTER SEVENTEEN

There was an early conference at Scotland Yard that morning under the chairmanship of Deputy Assistant Commissioner Napier. The only person missing was Nick, who was at Swallow House.

Lapham was still fuming about Herbert's disappearance which had been reported to him soon after its discovery in the early hours of the morning. What had happened was that the officer keeping the premises under observation had decided to check that Herbert was tucked up and asleep before slipping away to a nearby all-night coffee stall for a quarter of an hour. Accordingly, he had approached the night porter – whose main role was to ensure that late arrivals paid for their room before being given a key – and with the aid of a £1 tip and a story about being a reporter on an important assignment had persuaded him to go up to Herbert's room and make sure he was still there. If Herbert happened to be awake, he could easily say that he believed it was an unoccupied room.

As it was, of course, he returned to report that the room was empty and that there was no sign of Herbert. The officer concerned had then made his own search in the course of which he noticed the escape route which he reckoned Herbert had used.

When he telephoned the news to Scotland Yard, he had given himself the credit for having made the discovery earlier than might have been expected, without disclosing what had prompted him to make the check.

'It shows he's guilty,' Lapham said angrily. 'Why else should he disappear like that?'

'Guilty of what?' Wilcox enquired with a faint smile, peering over the top of his spectacles.

'If I catch him,' Lapham went on, ignoring the question, 'he'll find himself charged not only with blackmail but with perjury and perverting the course of justice *and* a few more things besides.'

'If someone thinks he's being tailed and doesn't want to be,' Napier remarked, 'it's the easiest thing on earth for him to shake it off, unless there's been time to mount a full-scale surveillance operation with radio contact and control points and the rest of it. We had neither the time nor the manpower to mount that sort of operation. Our only hope was that he wouldn't suspect he was being put under observation. Well, he obviously did and, for the time being, he's disappeared. Whether or not he reappears obviously depends on whether he's in any way involved in the blackmail. If he isn't, it wouldn't matter if we never heard of him again.'

'It would to me,' Lapham remarked.

'All right,' Napier said a trifle wearily, 'but let's move on and review other recent events. I gather that Thames Valley police have had no leads in tracing Farmer, assuming that Farmer is Mr X and that he was in Oxford for longer than was necessary to post a letter and a two pound packet of sugar. Incidentally, the lab say that there *was* an ounce of finely ground glass mixed with the sugar. They are also able to say that it was glass from a drinking vessel, as opposed to window glass or bottle glass. That's what their tests show.'

'By drinking vessel, you mean the sort of glass one drinks from?' Wilcox asked.

'I don't see what else they could mean. It must be that.' He put down the report he had been glancing at. 'The next matter is the phone call Sir Arnold Swallow received last night from his son. Unfortunately, we don't know where it came from. Trunk dialling may benefit the public, though sometimes I doubt it when you dial Edinburgh and get Penzance, but it's no help to us in tracing calls these days. Anyway, we know it was made by his son and that it was a demand for money. The sixty-four-thousand-dollar question is whether it was the instructions for payment promised in Mr X's last letter, i.e. is Sir Arnold's son Mr X?'

'I've spoken to W.P.C. Royston this morning,' Wilcox said. 'She seems a sensible, level-headed sort of girl and she says she had a distinct feeling that Swallow, young Swallow that is, was playing it by ear. That he was not speaking from what she called a prepared script. But, of course, that was only her impression.'

'Hmmm. It's possible the next half hour may shed light on that. What I have in mind is this. If Sir Arnold's mail this morning contains written instructions as to payment from Mr X, using his special code, then I think we can safely assume that Rupert Swallow is not Mr X, but that his intervention at this moment is fortuitous. If, on the other hand, no written demand arrives at Swallow House this morning, then maybe he is Mr X.' D.A.C. Napier scratched the lobe of one ear. 'Unhappily, we've not yet been able to trace him either.'

'Shall I phone Sergeant Attwell and see what the position is?' Wilcox asked.

'Yes, do that. The sooner we know the better.'

Using the D.A.C.'s telephone, Wilcox dialled Sir Arnold's private office number. He recognised Sir Arnold's voice as answering but, without wasting time on pleasantries, asked immediately for Nick.

'I was just about to phone, sir,' Nick said, as though reproached.

'That's all right, but what's the news?'

'No instructions about payment, but another letter card posted yesterday in Oxford which merely says, "Just in case you think I'm bluffing, you'll learn today that I'm not. Next time will be for real. Mr X." It's typed like the others, sir, and uses the red letter code.'

'What letter was it this time?'

'J. There's only one. The first letter of all.'

'Any idea what the note means?'

'No, sir. Mr Ralph Swallow was just making one or two enquiries in the building and then I was going to call you.'

'What sort of enquiries?'

'To find out whether anyone had received anything at all that might help to explain it.'

'I follow. O.K., Nick, I'll see you back here later,' Wilcox said, ringing off and turning to report to the others.

When he had finished, Napier observed with a sigh, 'We seem to be entirely dependent on other people's initiatives in this enquiry.'

Not more than half a mile from Scotland Yard stood the Victoria branch of H.Q. Supermarkets. The H.Q. stood for Highest Quality. And it was there that Mrs Fredericks did her twice weekly shopping, arriving soon after it opened at nine o'clock.

On this particular Wednesday morning, her wire basket was particularly heavy by the time she came round to the cash desk, as she had made additional purchases in preparation for a visit from her nephew.

With a heave, she lifted the basket of goods on to the counter and began to unpack them under the detached eye of the cashier.

The two pound packet of Swallow sugar was near the bottom and she took it out and deposited it on top of other purchases without looking at it. She was therefore surprised when the girl at the cash register suddenly seized it. For a second the girl stared at it with a puzzled expression.

'Where'd you get this?' she asked sharply.

'Here, of course,' Mrs Fredericks replied equally sharply as though fending off an accusation of misfeasance of some sort.

'What, over on the sugar shelf?'

'Yes. What are you on about?'

'Have you been writing on it?'

'Been writing on it? What are you talking about?'

'Look at this then.'

The girl turned the packet round so that Mrs Fredericks could see its other side. On the yellow paper of the packet was written in purple letters, 'Poisoned Sugar. Do not eat'.

Mrs Fredericks gave a gasp. 'Is this some sort of a joke?'

'It wasn't you who wrote that?'

'Of course it wasn't.'

'Hang on and I'll get the supervisor.'

Five minutes later, Mrs Fredericks found herself in the manager's office with the packet of sugar sitting on his desk between them.

'Do you recall exactly where this packet was in relation to other packets on the shelf?' the manager enquired.

'It was the nearest to hand, that's all I can tell you.'

'And you didn't notice any writing on it at that time?'

'The writing must have been on the far side otherwise I would have seen it.'

'And I gather you didn't notice the writing at all until the girl at the cash desk pointed it out?'

'Of course I didn't. You don't think I'd go and buy a packet of sugar marked poison, do you? It makes one wonder about your other stuff.'

'I'm sure that comment is quite unwarranted, Mrs Fredericks. We shall obviously have to notify the police and we shall, of course, replace the bag of sugar.'

'I'm not sure as I want any now. Not from your shop, anyway.'

'I would ask you most urgently, Mrs Fredericks, not to talk about this outside. At any rate, not until the police have investigated. I suspect it will prove to be no more than a hoax, though a hoax in the worst possible taste. Nevertheless I'm sure you will appreciate how damaging it could be for H.Q. Supermarkets if this sort of thing got out before there's been time to investigate and find the explanation.'

Mrs Fredericks stared at the packet of sugar for a while, then lifted her gaze to the manager's face. He was what she termed a smooth young man and she hadn't liked him at first.

She wasn't too sure she liked him any better now.

'But is it right that innocent people should run the risk of buying poisoned food here?' she asked. 'After all some of it may be poisoned without any warning on the packet.'

'I'm sure your good sense tells you that's most unlikely,' the manager said, feeling beads of sweat forming on his well shaved upper lip. 'After all, Mrs Fredericks, have you ever had cause for complaint before?'

'No. I've always found your stuff very good.'

'There you are then.'

'Though I shan't be too keen to shop here in future.'

'I'm sure my directors will be only too anxious to do anything they can to restore your confidence in H.Q. and to show their gratitude to you for your discretion in not spreading alarm about our shop. Anyway, it's time I phoned the police and then, of course, I must notify head office.' He gave Mrs Fredericks a sickly smile. 'I'm afraid it means your remaining here for a short while, but H.Q. will, of course, pay for your taxi fare home.' He gazed at the packet of sugar and shuddered. 'What a wicked, wicked hoax to play!'

Mrs Fredericks appeared not to hear him. Indeed, her mind had turned to the possibility of consulting a lawyer about the shock she had suffered. She wasn't a vindictive woman, but surely the law must provide for compensation when someone had had such an experience. And H.Q. Supermarkets were rich enough in all conscience.

It was about an hour later that Wilcox learnt of the incident and within five minutes he was at the scene.

Mrs Fredericks had by then been sent home in the promised taxi and her place in the manager's office had been taken by two directors from head office, who wore expressions of grim foreboding.

Also present was a Detective Sergeant from Rochester Row police station where the matter had been reported. He seemed both surprised and relieved by Wilcox's sudden arrival.

Without going into detail, Wilcox explained that there

seemed to be a link between this and an enquiry he was working on. To the obvious relief of the three H.Q. officials he
added that no other food was likely to have been tampered
with. He was informed in turn that every packet of sugar on
sale and in the stock room had been examined, but that none
had been found to bear the warning inscription on Mrs
Fredericks' packet.

'That means, someone planted that particular packet on the
shelf,' he said. 'Can we find out whether any of your staff
noticed anyone behaving in a suspicious manner near the
sugar shelf?'

'We've already checked on that, sir,' the detective sergeant
said, 'and drawn a blank.'

'There are always at least twenty people waiting to enter
when we open the doors at nine and they just swarm in,' the
manager remarked. 'It would have been quite easy for someone to plant it undetected.'

Wilcox had no difficulty believing this. Moreover, that it
applied to almost every supermarket in the country.

Mr X had put his message across very clearly.

The rowing was bad enough, but when they started throwing things about the room it was time to do something. There
had been a tremendous crash as an object shattered against
the bedroom door. In the immediate silence which followed
she had heard the man say, 'You're a vicious little kitten and
it's time I drew your claws.'

A few seconds later there was the sound of a slap and
the girl screamed out, 'Don't you dare touch me, you great ...'

The sentence remained unfinished, as the bed seemed
about to come clean through the wall.

Miss Pearman hesitated no longer but hastened to the phone
and dialled 999. On being connected with the police, she said
she believed a murder was being committed in her house.
No, it wasn't just a minor domestic disturbance, she replied
indignantly, so would they please hurry.

Within five minutes a patrol car drew up outside and a

couple of officers jumped out and strode purposefully to the front door.

'Are you the person who rang, madam?' the older one asked.

'Yes. It's my lodgers. They're in the back bedroom. I'm afraid he'll kill her if he hasn't already.'

The two officers darted upstairs with Miss Pearman behind. She pointed at a door. The older of the two officers turned the handle, but it was locked. He then banged on it heavily.

'What do you want?' Rupert Swallow called out.

'It's the police. Open up.'

'Why the hell should I? We don't need you.'

'Open the door or we'll force it.'

For a few seconds nothing happened and then a key was turned in the lock. The older officer immediately flung the door open and Miss Pearman peeped through from behind the safety of the two policemen.

There was a broken vase on the floor just inside the door. The man she knew as Mr Armitage was glaring angrily at the officers while the girl, who looked dishevelled, was sitting on the bed with her knees pulled up to her chin and staring at the door with a mixture of alarm and bewilderment.

'Are you all right?' the older officer asked her. She nodded her head. 'Has he been assaulting you?'

'We just had a bit of a row, that's all,' Swallow remarked.

'It sounded more like you were killing her,' Miss Pearman put in. 'I heard her scream, too.'

'Well, you can see I haven't killed her,' Swallow said abrasively. 'So perhaps you'll now all clear out and leave us alone.'

'Seems you're very keen for us to go,' the older officer said in a challenging tone. 'Did he cause that bruise beneath your left eye?' he asked, looking in the direction of the girl again.

She felt her cheek and then gazed at her hand.

'Look, do you mind leaving us alone,' Swallow interjected. 'We haven't done anything which requires your presence in our bedroom.'

'I don't want them staying on here,' Miss Pearman said.

'I shan't feel safe till they leave.'

'We're leaving anyway.'

'I still want a few particulars,' the older officer said stubbornly.

It was at this point that Rupert Swallow, whose anger had been smouldering fiercely, gave the officer a push in the chest with the palm of his hand as if to eject him from the room.

The younger officer immediately slipped round behind him and pinioned his arms.

'I'm arresting you for assaulting a police officer in the execution of his duty,' the older man said in a tone of satisfaction.

The girl who had remained in a hunched position on the bed suddenly leapt to her feet.

'I might have guessed it would end like this,' she shouted at Swallow. 'You and your promises and all your big talk about Florida. The nearest you're ever going to get to Florida is a police station. Well, don't expect to find me still around when you get back.' She gave an angry toss of her head. 'To think I was ever taken in by all your smooth promises. I must have been crazy.'

'Not crazy, kitten,' he replied in a vicious tone, 'just a go-getting little slut.'

Miss Pearman let out a gasp while the officer holding Swallow bundled him through the door and down the stairs.

On arrival at the police station he was placed in a cell and informed he would be interviewed when he had had time to cool off.

In the course of this process he decided that there was no point in further antagonising the police and that, if he co-operated from now on, there was every chance of his being dealt with in Court the next day and receiving a small fine. After all, it had been a very minor assault and anyone could see that he was in a temper at the time. Not with the officer, but with that tantalising little bitch who was the cause of all the trouble.

Accordingly, when he was fetched from his cell a couple of

hours later, he was as amenable as he had been the reverse two hours earlier.

'Did you say your name was Swallow?' the sergeant said, suspiciously.

'That's right.'

'I was told it was Armitage.'

'Rupert Armitage Swallow.'

'Well, I'm damned,' the sergeant said, staring at him disbelievingly.

'What's up then?'

'You'll find out soon enough. As if you didn't know,' he added.

Forty-five minutes later, Wilcox and Nick arrived at the police station and Rupert Swallow was once more fetched from his cell. He gave the two officers a quizzical look as he sat down.

After introducing themselves, Wilcox said, 'Would I be right in thinking that you telephoned your father last night?'

'Yes. There was no secret about it.'

'You say that, but you nevertheless refused to tell him where you were speaking from. Isn't that so?'

'True. But if you know so much, you presumably also know that my father and I are not exactly on the best of terms. I saw no need to tell him my whereabouts.'

'For what reason did you call him?'

'For money, as you obviously know.'

'A very large sum of money.'

'Yes.'

'What did you mean when you told your father you didn't think he would dare refuse your demand?'

Rupert Swallow made a face and shrugged. 'It was just a bit of bluff to try and persuade him. As a matter of fact I hadn't intended saying it, but he sounded odd last night. Nervy, jumpy, unlike his usual self, so I saw no reason not to make him a bit jumpier still.'

'What were you proposing to do if he didn't meet your demand?'

146

'Bugger all.' He gave a harsh laugh. 'I wish there was something I could do to squeeze money out of him. Any suggestions?'

Wilcox ignored the question and went on, 'Do you have a typewriter?'

'No.'

'Can you type?'

'Painfully with one finger.'

'And what about your girl-friend?'

'Her? Use a typewriter? Not unless she'd heard they had sexual possibilities. Anyway, what are all these questions in aid of?'

'Would it be fair to say you hate your father?'

'I certainly don't like him. I have no reason to.'

'Would you like to see him ruined?'

'I haven't thought about it. There doesn't seem much chance of it, anyway. Thanks to the nation's sweet tooth, he's rolling in money.'

'Do you feel vindictive towards him?'

'I've said I don't like him.'

'I'm asking if you would like to see him hurt? Hurt in his business life?'

'I think I could survive the grief,' Swallow said, with a twisted sort of smile. 'After all, he's cut me out of his life and out of his will, so I've got nothing to lose if the company goes bust. Though I can't see that happening.'

'But you'd like it to?'

'I've already told you my feelings on the subject. Isn't it about time you told me the purpose of all these questions? Obviously my father reported my call last night to the police, but why? I've asked him for money before without his bringing your lot in. So what was so special about last night's call?'

'It was for a very large sum and it was accompanied by threats?'

'What threats?'

'The veiled threat that something disagreeable would happen if he dared refuse you this time.'

147

'I've told you that was just a bit of bluff. Opportunism, if you like, because I thought he sounded jumpy. It seemed he might be more vulnerable to a request than he usually is.'

'Some might call it blackmail rather than a request.'

'Absolute bollocks.'

'Have you ever written anonymous letters to your father?'

'I haven't written him letters of any sort since I was at boarding school.'

'Have you sent him letters at Swallow House in Baker Street?'

'Refer to last answer.'

Wilcox frowned slightly. 'We shall get on better if you answer my questions properly.'

'All right, then. No, I haven't.'

'Have you ever *caused* letters to be sent to him there?'

'No.'

'Have you ever referred to yourself as Mr X?'

'No. Nor as Mr Y or Mr Z or any other letter of the bloody alphabet.'

Wilcox turned towards Nick and raised an eyebrow. 'Anything else to ask him?'

Nick shook his head. He was as satisfied, as he was sure Wilcox must also be, that Rupert Armitage had nothing to do with Mr X's demands on Swallow Sugar. Here was one suspect who could now be eliminated from the enquiry.

'All right, that's all we want to ask you for the time being,' Wilcox remarked.

'Aren't you going to tell me what this is all about?'

'I'm not telling you anything.'

'Am I free to go now?'

'That's not for me to say. You were brought here for assaulting a police officer. I imagine you'll be charged with that offence, but it's not my decision.'

Wilcox and Nick stood up and Swallow did likewise, looking at them both with an expression of ill-concealed hostility.

'Thank you for nothing,' he said. 'And if you happen to see my father, don't bother to give him my regards.'

As they were driving back to the Yard, Nick said, 'I felt a bit sorry for him in some ways. I don't know that I'd want to have Sir Arnold Swallow as a father.'

'I'm darned sure I shouldn't,' Wilcox replied. 'But then I'm equally sure I shouldn't want Master Rupert as a son.'

The remainder of the day passed without further developments.

When Nick got home that evening and told Clare all that had happened, she said, 'I felt all along that Rupert Swallow was a red herring.'

'I know. You said so. What do you make of Herbert's disappearance?'

She shook her head slowly from side to side. 'There's something very puzzling about his whole trial.'

'As though it was all a charade.'

'Yes, exactly that.'

CHAPTER EIGHTEEN

At first Miss Gunn did not recognise the envelope as she glanced quickly through Sir Arnold's mail the next morning. This was because her eye was on the look-out for a letter card with an Oxford postmark.

But the deception lasted only a second or two as she realised that a long manila envelope bearing a London postmark had had the address typed on the now familiar machine.

As soon as she came through the door into his room, Sir Arnold could tell from her expression that Mr X had communicated again.

She handed him the letter separately from the others and watched him anxiously as he slit open one end and extracted a large sheet of flimsy airmail paper.

He shook it open, rather than unfold it, so as to avoid leaving his own fingerprints on the surface. This was something Nick had told him to do.

In a rare gesture of solidarity, he motioned Miss Gunn to come round beside him so that she could read it for herself. It was as if he did not wish to read it alone. The letter ran:

'Dear Sir, I suppose it was inevitable that you would go to the police even though I'd warned you not to. Anyway, you must now pay for your foolishness. And I mean *pay*. I now require £150,000 instead of my original more modest demand. Not that an extra £50,000 will make much difference to Swallow Sugar. But it will make a big difference to me so perhaps I ought to thank you for your foolishness. And the police won't be able to protect your money anyway. By now you'll know that I'm a man of my word. So it's £150,000 I want OR. Here are your instructions. (1) Have the money in used £10 notes. (2) Wrap it in a waterproof sheet. (3) Pack the money into one of those plastic open-top boxes – you may need two of them. And having done that wait for further instructions. I will give you 24 hours to comply. Any time after that expect final instructions which must be obeyed *immediately* if we are to avoid any nasty accidents later. If they are not obeyed immediately, you know what to expect and there won't be any warning on the next packet – or should I say packets. Yours faithfully, Mr. X.'

Though the letter made no mention of any code, each 'k' was typed in red. By this time, however, Mr X had no need to use his code for his letters to be identified.

Miss Gunn gave a small shiver as she finished reading it.

'I never believed such terrible people existed,' she said. 'He's just like a torturer.'

'I'll call Detective Chief Superintendent Wilcox straightaway,' Sir Arnold said.

But before he could reach for the cream-coloured phone which was his direct line to the outside world, it started to ring.

'Yes, good morning, I was about to call you ... yes, we have had a letter ... yes, I'll be here when you come ... yes, all right in half an hour.'

'As you'll have gathered, that was the police. They wish to see me, anyway. They have some news for me.'

'I'll make sure they're brought up as soon as they arrive,' Miss Gunn said, turning to go.

In fact, Wilcox and Nick arrived in something less than half an hour. Sir Arnold was at his desk reading Mr X's letter for the umpteenth time as they entered his office. He pointed at it without saying a word and got up, so that the officers could read it where it lay. While they were doing so, he went across and gazed stonily out of the window.

'Is this the envelope?' Wilcox asked.

Sir Arnold turned. 'Yes.'

'So Mr X has come back to London,' Wilcox remarked. 'Posted yesterday. Envelope has a slightly grubby and crumpled look as though it had been carried around a while before being posted.'

'It could have happened in the post, sir,' Nick said.

'Could have, but I'd guess not. You can usually tell between something that's been roughly treated in transit and something that was already a bit soiled when it was put into the post. My observation tells me this was the latter. So what do we deduce from that I wonder?'

'That it wasn't posted near Mr X's home but was carried about in his pocket.'

Wilcox nodded. 'Whatever else he may be, he's also a sadist. Not only is the nature of his threat sadistic, but the tone of his letters indicate that as well.'

'Also the way he's spinning the whole thing out,' Nick added.

'Which brings us back to Farmer,' Wilcox said. 'He's the one person in our sights whose motive could include a streak of sadism.' He paused and shrugged. 'Anyway, we're obviously nearing the climax.' He looked across at Sir Arnold who was still standing over by the window. 'Can you get the money within the next few hours?'

'I can make the necessary arrangements with the bank.'

'I think you should.'

'Don't you sometimes on these occasions use paper cut to the size of treasury notes?' he asked in a tight voice.

'It depends on the operation,' Wilcox said. 'We've obviously got to stake our all on catching Mr X red-handed. In which case you'll have your money back. But we have to face the possibility of failure, in which event Swallow Sugar would have to face the very real threat of contaminated sugar being distributed around the country if Mr X merely found himself with a load of waste paper instead of £150,000. I think he's provided us with enough evidence that he's able and ready to carry out his threat if he's thwarted. As I say, our best hope is going to be to catch him as he collects.'

'I hope you can,' Sir Arnold remarked grimly.

'None of the previous letters have provided us with finger-prints or scientific clues of any sort and I don't imagine this one will prove to be an exception,' Wilcox said staring at the letter, 'but we'd better have it examined right away.' He frowned. 'Money to be wrapped in waterproof covering and packed in an open-top plastic container,' he mused. 'What can we deduce from that?'

'That the hand-over involves the probability of immersion in water.'

'Something like that, but what? He must know that wherever it's left we're going to be watching like hawks for someone to come and pick it up. That's always the blackmailer's moment of greatest danger, when he goes to collect the loot. That's when he's invariably nicked. And our Mr X must know that as well as anyone. He's been pretty clever so far and we must obviously credit him with having devised as foolproof a scheme for collection as his subtle mind is capable of.'

'My guess is that we shall be told to leave it in one place and he'll collect it somewhere else,' Nick said.

'How do you mean?'

'I think the next lot of instructions will say that a long piece of rope must be attached to the box and left in a certain way so that he can tow it away under cover.' Nick paused. 'I know that doesn't sound very plausible, but it must be something on those lines.'

'Hmm!' Wilcox sounded unconvinced. 'It's obviously something fairly elaborate. It has to be ... Supposing it's to be dropped by plane ... No, wait a moment, lowered from a helicopter in some bit of countryside after dark. Supposing it was that, we'd have the hell of a job catching the fellow, assuming he didn't give us much notice.'

'The company owns a light plane,' Sir Arnold said, like someone tossing a pebble into a pool.

'Where's it kept?'

'At Luton.'

'I suppose all your employees know of its existence?'

'Certainly. But it wouldn't be any good for jettisoning something into a given area. It's a twin-engined jet and much too fast for that sort of operation.'

'Mr X mightn't know that. A lot of people don't realise you can't just lob things out of a modern jet the way you could out of an open cockpit First World War plane.'

'I doubt whether our Mr X would make that sort of mistake,' Nick said.

'So do I,' Wilcox replied with a slow nod. 'But it doesn't knock out the helicopter possibility. Indeed, it could be just the sort of elaborate scheme he might think up.'

Nick tried to envisage the scene. Some lonely piece of countryside with no ready access roads and Mr X hiding in the dark waiting for the helicopter to arrive overhead and lower the money. But how would he guide it to the exact spot he wanted? Presumably by displaying some luminous sign. Nick's mind turned to the problem which would then face him in getting away from the scene. He would have to have a car parked somewhere in the vicinity and then drive like a bat out of hell to get clear away before the police could close in on the ground. Assuming he had chosen the site carefully, this might not present a great problem. And if there was one thing which Mr X had demonstrated, it was an ability to plan with care and not to rush his fences.

He was still envisaging a scene which more and more resembled the climax of a T.V. serial when he heard Sir Arnold speak.

'You said on the phone that you had something you wished to speak to me about?'

'That's right,' Wilcox said. 'We've traced and interviewed your son. As a result we're satisfied that he's not Mr X.'

Sir Arnold, whose expression became unrelievedly severe, asked in a taut voice, 'Where did you find him?'

'There was a disturbance at a house where he and a girl were staying. Police were called. He made a minor assault on one of the officers and was arrested. When they got him to the station, it was realised who he was and I was informed.'

'Where is he now?'

'He's coming up in Court this morning on the assault charge. After that he'll be a free man as far as we're concerned.' Wilcox paused. 'I didn't think you'd want to know and he was anxious that you shouldn't be told anyway.'

'I see.'

'But it was clear that he knew nothing about the present blackmail attempt.'

'At least I can be thankful for that.'

'The money he asked you for on the phone the night before last was to support him and the girl in America.'

'So I realise.' He gave the two officers a haggard look. 'If either of you two gentlemen have sons, I hope you will be spared the worry I have had as a father.'

Nick thought of Master Attwell and then of all the boys he'd come across in his job who had gone off the rails in one way or another. With all the pride and excitement welling within him at the prospect of imminent fatherhood, it was impossible to envisage himself with an estranged son.

It was just after Sir Arnold had spoken in private to his bank manager that Miss Gunn came hurrying into the room with a letter.

'This was delivered by hand about five minutes ago,' she said breathlessly. 'It was handed to the man on the door by a youth who simply said he'd been asked to deliver it.'

One glance at the envelope was sufficient for them to see that it was one of Mr X's missives.

He's getting bolder, thought Nick as he watched Sir Arnold opening it. After reading it, Sir Arnold passed it to Wilcox, who held it for Nick to read at the same time.

'Dear Sir Arnold,' it read, 'This will reach you by hand, though not my hand nor the hand of anyone who knows me, so don't waste your time or the time of the police in trying to follow that up. The only reason for sending it this way is to remind you once again how vulnerable you are. How close I can get to you without your knowing what'll happen next. You're like a man hearing sounds in the dark all round him but never knowing where the next will come from. I hope you got my letter this morning with instructions about how to pack up the money. Having got it ready, you must take it with you wherever you go so that you can act on my next instructions without a second's delay. So much is going to depend on your doing that. If you haven't had instructions by the time you leave your office tomorrow, you must take the money home. Poor old Mason will lift it in and out of the car for you. What's more you should cancel any engagement you have for tomorrow evening and drive straight home from the office and stay in all the evening. Yours faithfully, Mr. X.'

When they had finished reading, Wilcox and Nick looked at each other.

'Are you thinking what I'm thinking?' Wilcox asked.

'You mean the mention of Mason by name?'

'Exactly. It's the first time Mr X has dropped a clue that he's an inside man. Who but an employee or an ex-employee would know that Mason is Sir Arnold's chauffeur? We can even narrow it. So it can't just be any old employee, but one who knows the routine at Swallow House.'

'That can only mean Farmer,' Nick observed.

'Precisely,' Wilcox said emphatically.

Jeffrey Farmer was feeling restive. Since his return from Oxford he had been staying in a boarding-house in the Shepherd's Bush area which was convenient but uncomfortable. Its chief virtue was that the couple who ran it – and, incidentally, made a nice profit out of doing so – knew better than to be inquisitive about their guests. It certainly was not the sort of establishment where the owner passed bits of information to the police. In fact the reverse, in the sense that if he told them anything at all it would be with the intention of misleading them.

To that extent, therefore, Farmer felt safer than he had done in either Reading or Oxford, where he was at the mercy of nosy landladies.

He knew that the police were looking for him and it was

this, coupled with all the delay, that was making him restive.

On top of which Minnie Dove had told him not to telephone her at *The Three Ducks* any more. She had warned him of her fear that the police might be tapping her phone in the hope of incriminating him. Accordingly, all he had been able to do was to let her know where he was staying and leave it to her to get in touch with him.

He was grateful to her for her staunch support and looked forward to rewarding her for her kindness in the none too distant future.

In the meantime, however, he still had important things to attend to ...

It was good to think that Sir Arnold Swallow was in a sweat; better still that he would soon be in an even greater one.

Herbert Sipson, on the other hand, was feeling right on top of the world. In a life of ups and downs, with more failures than successes, he had nevertheless remained indomitably optimistic that one day he would bring off a major coup of the sort that, years later, would be talked about by the connoisseurs. He now felt that day was near. And its prospect filled him with bubbling satisfaction.

Since slipping away from the Beasley Hotel, he had taken a room in Earls Court. With its floating population of long-haired young and melancholy-eyed itinerants, he was afforded the degree of unquestioned anonymity he sought.

It was not that he felt himself on the run from the police as he was quite certain he would not be arrested even if he was recognised. The worst that would happen would be a renewal of the surveillance which he had been at pains to slip. But as he did not want to have the trouble of slipping it again – and it would undoubtedly be harder next time – it was preferable to merge with the sort of background that Earls Court provided.

All this passed through his mind as he sat in a café with an undrunk cup of tea on the table in front of him. He was still relishing his release from custody and reflecting how prison always seemed worse in retrospect.

When he was part of its system, he became inured to the constant shouting of the officers, the terrible echoing sound of clanging metal, the long hours of sheer boredom and the suppression of personal choice. It was only afterwards he realised how awful it had been each time.

He was determined not to land up in prison again. Bad luck had been his undoing in the past. He could not believe that bad luck would continue to dog his footsteps. And so far the omens were excellent.

He picked up his cup and blew on the tea before taking a sip. Then grimacing slightly he reached for the sugar and took a further two lumps. He gazed reflectively for a second at the bright yellow wrapping with a small soaring swallow on each of its six sides, before dropping the sugar into his cup and crumpling the paper.

His glance went round the eight tables. On each was a bowl containing Swallow lump sugar. Herbert frowned. It seemed the company had an absolute monopoly. And Herbert who regarded himself as a small man in a big, grasping world did not approve of monopolies. Or so he was able to persuade himself at this moment.

He looked at his watch and drank the rest of his tea.

It was time to leave and keep an important appointment.

Mr Stavering, who was the laboratory's expert in the examination of documents, had not taken long to establish that Mr X's latest letter had been typed on the same machine as all the others.

He now carried the letter over to a work bench and carefully placed it in a polythene envelope to preserve it. From a drawer he took all the previous letters received from Mr X, including that sent to the Shangri-La Bingo Company, and lined them up on the bench in front of him.

For several minutes his gaze went from one to the next and then back again. It was a gaze of concentrated thought and his brow was furrowed in a deep frown as he made his study.

Like all experts, who are liable to be called to give evidence in Court as to their conclusions, he never voiced an opinion until he was satisfied he could stand by it under cross-examination. Failure to observe this somewhat obvious precept could not only lead to the destruction of the prosecution's case but, far worse, to the professional discredit of the expert concerned.

For some time Bob Stavering had been forming a view about the letters; a view which had been strengthened by his examination of each successive letter. And now strengthened to the point of certainty by his examination of the one which Nick had handed him only an hour earlier.

The fact that Nick had been able to hand it to him personally was an indication of the urgency and gravity with which the whole investigation was being treated. Normally, material delivered at the laboratory for examination was received and signed for by liaison officers so that the experts themselves were not interrupted in their work in the lab's various departments.

Stavering now took the first and last letters from their respective polythene envelopes and carried them over to a sort of microscope on an adjoining bench.

For several minutes, he examined each in turn. Then he held them up to his nose and sniffed. He had always been a great believer that a scientist should not ignore his own primary senses, which there was a tendency to do as more and more items of technical equipment filled the laboratory and performed much of the work done previously by the expert's naked eye or his taste buds or his nose.

Having completed his examination, he paused once more in deep thought before walking over to a small cubicle of an office in one corner of the room.

He sat down at the desk and, reaching for the telephone, dialled Wilcox's extension at Scotland Yard.

'Stavering here, Chief Superintendent,' he said when Wilcox answered. 'I've just finished examining the letter Sergeant Attwell brought a short time ago. I doubt whether there's anything I can tell you about it you won't have guessed. Typed on the same machine. No fingerprints, I gather.' He paused. 'But I've just been looking at all the letters again and I've come to two conclusions. The first is that they were all typed at about the same time.'

'I don't think that helps very much. After all, they've been received over a period of a week and I imagine that would cover what you mean by "about the same time"?'

Stavering waited until Wilcox had finished. Then he said, 'When I say *all*, I'm including the one sent to the Shangri-La Bingo Company.'

For a few seconds there was a stunned silence at the other end of the line. Wilcox's tone was wary when he next spoke.

'Are you saying that they were all typed several months ago?'

'In my view, yes.'

'Because that's what it must mean.'

'Exactly.'

'Well, thanks for the information. It throws a whole new light on the case.'

'I realise that. It's one of the reasons I didn't want to say anything until I was sure. But my examination of this final letter has lifted it out of the realm of speculation and put it in that of scientific deduction.'

'But how do you account for the fact that the letters to Swallow Sugar appear to be in reply to the company's own responses?' Wilcox's tone rang with the sort of doubt that longed to be assuaged if that were possible. He went on, 'I mean the second letter referred to the advertisement inserted in the *Evening Standard* and this last one refers to the fact that the company have gone to the police, how do you reconcile that with what you now say?'

Stavering gave a dry laugh. 'Those are not scientific questions. The contents of the letters are not for my interpretation. But since you ask me the question, couldn't the answer be intelligent anticipation? It was a reasonable bet that the company would make contact in the manner required; also that they'd immediately report the matter to the police. I would have thought it was fairly safe to have prepared letters in advance on that assumption. After all, they didn't have to be posted if the assumptions turned out to be wrong.'

'Those are good points,' Wilcox said, thoughtfully. He sighed and added in a tone which was not intended to sound reproachful, 'It's an awful pity you weren't in a position to tell us that while Sipson was still on trial.'

'I daresay, but it's only the fact that this last letter has been typed on the same sort of paper as the one to the Shangri-La Bingo Company that has enabled me to reach the conclusion. The first letter to Swallow Sugar was on different paper and the next two, as you will recall, were stamped letter cards.' He paused. 'Anyway, I'll let you have my report as soon as anyone can be found to type it.'

Clare put down the paper she had been reading and lay back in her chair.

Two days after Herbert Sipson's trial had ended, it might never have been. Not that it had ever achieved all that amount of publicity until it had gone into camera and that was near enough the end, anyway. The public, and the press which fed it, had become so sated with crime that only the most original and spectacular cases made regular news.

The first day of Herbert's trial had been reported, but thereafter less and less had appeared in the paper until the press found themselves banned from the proceedings. Then there had been a blaze of publicity for the judge's decision, including a number of critical leading articles. But that had died down as quickly as it had flared up so that the end of the case went largely unnoticed. It was as if the press, having been earlier spurned, was determined to take no interest in the outcome.

What struck Clare as she now thought about this was that there had been no leaks to the press about the reason for the 'in camera' proceedings. In particular, she would have expected Herbert himself to have volunteered the information for a price. It was a good story for some enterprising reporter.

But there had not been so much as a breath of publicity of the unfolding drama at Swallow Sugar and Clare could not believe that Herbert of all people had been deterred by the judge's strictures about contempt of court. In any case, there was no real risk involved, newspaper sources of information being as diligently and deviously guarded as the inner councils of the Kremlin itself.

So there had to be another reason and the only one which came to Clare was that Herbert did not consider that his own interests would be served by such publicity. And the only possible reason for his taking that line was because he was himself heavily involved in what was happening.

On no fewer than three previous occasions he had been convicted of blackmail. And each time his downfall, according to Nick, had been an over-elaborate scheme. Well, elaborateness was certainly the hall-mark of the Shangri-La Bingo case and even more so of that concerning Swallow Sugar.

She sat suddenly bolt upright as a further line of thought entered her head.

If at first blush it seemed implausible, it was at least logical. And not merely logical; it fitted in with everything that had happened.

Bob Stavering's recent conclusion would, moreover, had Clare been aware of it, have confirmed the theory which had emerged from its chrysalis in her mind.

Sir Arnold Swallow had left the building to be driven home and Miss Gunn had just covered the typewriter for the night when the phone rang in her office.

'I want to speak to Sir Arnold Swallow,' a strangely muffled voice said.

'I'm afraid Sir Arnold has left. Can I give him a message in the morning?'

'Just tell him it won't be long now before he gets his desserts, the cheating old bastard.'

Miss Gunn found herself recording the message on her

shorthand pad before the full implications of the call struck her.

'Yes, hold on,' she said desperately. If she could raise the girl on their exchange on the internal phone, it might be possible to trace the caller.

'You've got that, have you?' the voice asked.

'I wonder if you could just repeat it,' Miss Gunn said valiantly. 'I'm afraid it's not a very good connection.'

'You heard enough,' the voice replied. 'And anyway, deeds speak louder than words. It won't be long now, tell him.'

'Are you Mr X?' Miss Gunn asked, in a voice hoarse with nervousness. At least his answer should establish something, she felt.

'Of course I'm Mr X,' he said after a pause and then he laughed. Immediately afterwards he rang off.

It was with chagrin Miss Gunn later learnt from Stephanie on their switchboard that it had not been possible to trace the call, though it had definitely been made from a public call box.

She was, however, commended by Wilcox for her efforts when she phoned him a few minutes later.

All she could really say was that it was a male voice, that it was plainly disguised and that it was not one which she recognised.

'All part of the softening up process being carried out by Mr X, I suppose,' Wilcox remarked to Nick. 'And yet curiously out of pattern.'

Nick nodded. 'Much more like that call Sir Arnold got at home last week.'

'Yes,' Wilcox said in a thoughtful tone and went on, 'It seems that Mr X is a split personality. Or perhaps that he wants to give that impression. I wonder why?'

CHAPTER NINETEEN

The bright orange container sitting in a corner of Sir Arnold's office hypnotised him. He found his gaze constantly returning to it. Into the container had been fitted the carefully wrapped parcel of £10 notes. Fifteen thousand of them in neat bundles. The inner wrapping consisted of a sheet of plastic, the outer covering was an old army mackintosh ground sheet. The package filled the orange container to within about five inches of its open top.

In amongst the notes had been concealed a small electronic device which was already transmitting signals.

'I just hope it works when it comes to it,' Wilcox had remarked dubiously. 'I never trust these cute toys.'

'It'll either win the day single-handed or be an utter failure,' D.A.C. Napier had replied.

The expert who had been called in to advise on this aspect had said tartly, 'If there's any failure, you can be sure it'll be human failure.'

Although Swallow House gave every appearance of normal routine to the casual observer on this anticipated D-day, it had become a sensitive command headquarters behind the façade of business as usual.

A number of unmarked police cars were in position in neighbouring streets, one of them detailed to shadow Sir Arnold's Rolls wherever it went that day.

A keen-eyed plain-clothes officer lounged casually near the commissionaire's desk at the main entrance.

Two more officers were keeping Stephanie company on the switchboard, ready to intercept any suspicious calls.

Upstairs on the seventh floor, Nick sat in a corner of Miss Gunn's room with a telephone line permanently open to Scotland Yard.

Meanwhile, alone in his own office, Sir Arnold tried to work but found his attention always returning to the bright orange box in the corner. He felt it was like sitting in a room with a nuclear bomb. In each case, the harmless appearance only added to the sinister implications.

It had, of course, been necessary to give some sort of cover story to those members of the staff whose routine was affected by the arrangements. They had all appeared quite satisfied by the explanation that a bomb threat had been received and that, though the police believed it to be a hoax, no chances were being taken. Nevertheless the importance of not discussing the matter was stressed. Luckily those like Mason, the chauffeur, the commissionaire and Stephanie had all been with the company for many years and were loyal employees who accepted the situation without asking awkward questions.

And so the morning at Swallow House dragged by. There had been no further communications from Mr X in the post and by twelve o'clock nothing had happened.

'Perhaps he's realised he'll never get away with it,' Miss Gunn remarked to Nick in a hopeful tone. 'Perhaps all he wanted to do was create as much worry and confusion as he could.'

'I doubt it,' Nick replied. 'It has all the appearance of blackmail on a colossal scale.'

'I don't know what the world is coming to,' Miss Gunn remarked. She belonged to a generation from whose lips this cry was frequently heard. 'I can only think that whoever it is must be mad.'

Nick smiled. 'No madder than you or I, Miss Gunn. Just greedier, that's all.'

'Poor Sir Arnold! I don't think anyone realises what a strain he's been under this past week.'

Nick made no reply. He was not disposed to accord the

chairman of Swallow Sugar more than formal sympathy at the most.

'The company means everything to him,' Miss Gunn went on. 'It's his whole life. If this terrible threat were ever carried out, I really believe it would kill him.'

Nick felt obliged to nod, even though he doubted that anything of the sort would happen. The Sir Arnolds of this life were, in his limited experience, a tough and durable species who invariably survived when others succumbed.

About one o'clock, Miss Gunn took her boss a pot of tea and two rounds of ham sandwiches. She then made a further pot of tea which she shared with Nick who had, with foresight, brought his own sandwiches with him.

It was while he was eating them that Wilcox came through on the open line.

'Still all quiet at your end?'

'Nothing to report at all,' Nick said.

'Frankly, I didn't expect anything to happen during the day. It'll be this evening after dark that events will move.'

'I agree that's much more likely, sir.'

'How's Sir Arnold?'

'I only catch glimpses of him when Miss Gunn goes in to his office.'

'There's still no trace of Farmer,' Wilcox said.

'Nor of Sipson, I take it?'

'No. But we're not officially looking for him, of course. If he is involved, we'll catch him then. The D.A.C. didn't feel we'd be justified in putting out a call for him at this stage. I think he's nervous about the rumpus there could be if he *is* completely innocent. Re-arrest of a recently acquitted man and all that. You know what the press could make of it. Anyway, we've more or less given up hope of pinching Mr X's scheme in the bud. The idea now is to concentrate all our efforts on catching him at the moment of collection. That's when he's going to have to expose himself.' He paused. 'If we fail then, God help us.'

'Anything being done about Minnie Dove, sir?'

'Yes, I've got someone keeping an eye on her place, but so far she seems to be spending a blameless day. I've done my best to ensure that she doesn't receive communications of any sort without our being aware of their contents. Incidentally, I did hear from one of the local officers this morning that she is reputed to be heavily in debt. Owes money all round the place.'

'So £150,000 wouldn't come amiss?'

'I gather she's open to any contributions.'

'It could be she and Farmer are in harness.'

'Could very possibly be so.'

After Wilcox had rung off, Nick went on eating his sandwiches. Miss Gunn had gone out of the room and so his thoughts were undisturbed by her anxious presence.

Clare was sure that Herbert was the key to the whole affair and supported her view with logical argument. Nick agreed that Herbert was involved in some way, but he thought he was more a decoy than a main protagonist. Possibly even an unwitting decoy. That would mean that Farmer and Minnie Dove had devised a scheme using Herbert's original crime and trial for their own purposes. This seemed a tenable theory, particularly if Herbert was to receive a pay-off for his role as decoy. But against that, there was absolutely no evidence to connect Herbert with either Farmer or Minnie Dove.

It was at that moment that Wilcox rang again.

'When you went down to Brixton prison last week, weren't you told that Sipson mentioned a sister-in-law who would have visited him if she hadn't lived too far away?'

'That's right, sir.'

'That's what I thought. I've just been going through the pile of statements that have been taken and there's one from a prison officer who made a report on Sipson the evening after Swallow Sugar had received the first letter. You remember we asked the prison authorities to keep their eyes and ears especially well open?'

'Yes, I spoke to Chief Officer Gillam, sir.'

'Well, there's nothing remarkable about this chap's statement – indeed, it's merely a recital of chit-chat between Sipson and a prisoner named Japp while they were having a game of draughts – save for the fact that Sipson appears to have mentioned that his only family was an older brother who was a widower ...'

'Then how could he have a sister-in-law?' Nick broke in.

'How indeed?'

CHAPTER TWENTY

A few minutes after five o'clock, a cheery-looking lad of about ten trotted through the main entrance of Swallow House and approached the commissionaire.

' 'Ere you are,' he said with a cheeky smile, skimming an envelope across the desk.

The police officer then on duty was at the commissionaire's side almost before he could pick it up. It was addressed to Sir Arnold Swallow and marked 'Private and Extremely Urgent' in the top left hand corner.

Without a word, the officer bounded out of the building in time to see the boy standing at the kerb about a dozen yards away waiting to cross. Before he had time to do so, the officer had reached him.

'Come back inside a minute, I want a word with you,' the officer said, putting a hand on the boy's arm.

The boy's expression changed to one of alarm. 'What's wrong?' he asked. 'I ain't done nothing.'

'What's your name, son?' the officer said, as he steered the unresisting boy back towards Swallow House.

'Andrew.'

'Andrew who?'

'Andrew King.'

'Where'd that letter come from?'

'An old man asked me to take it.'

'What old man?'

'I dunno. Back down the road about five minutes ago. 'E 'ad a stick and said 'e was all tired and as I was going that way, would I deliver it. That's all I done.'

'Did he give you anything?'

'Yea, 20p.'

'What'd he look like?'

''Ad a grey beard and a stick cos he limped bad.'

'Would you recognise him again?'

'Might do.'

It was while Andrew King was still being questioned in a room on the ground floor that the letter he had delivered reached Sir Arnold, who opened it while Nick stood immediately behind him so that he could read it at the same time.

On this occasion there was no 'dear sir' and its content was peremptory and businesslike.

> 'Leave within five minutes of opening this letter,' it ran. 'Drive to West Drayton Railway Station, then to Honey Lane half a mile from there. In Honey Lane there is a hollow oak opposite the transformer station. Obtain further instructions from oak. Now, hurry. Mr. X.'

Each letter 'm' was typed in red. Mr X was still punctilious about identifying himself even if he had curbed his style of letter-writing.

Nick could not remember a five minutes into which he had packed so much activity. There was a call to Wilcox; calls to alert the waiting cars below; instructions to the officer interviewing the boy and to those on the switchboard.

And yet in little over five minutes he was in a car pulling away behind Sir Arnold's from Swallow House. The evening traffic was already building up and it was some time before they were bowling along Westway in the direction of the White City. Ahead of them was the Rolls driven by Mason with Sir Arnold alone in the darkened rear. On the floor at his feet lay the orange box containing the money. A rug had been thrown over it to hide it from any inquisitive gaze.

After the White City they were in heavy traffic again as they threaded their way along the Uxbridge Road.

For most of the journey Nick pored over a map. He found Honey Lane. It was east of the railway station and appeared to fizzle out close to the main line which ran along an embankment at that point.

It was a strange amorphous area of factories, housing estates and open countryside. An area where London's western suburbs merged with one another, though leaving pockets of open land.

Honey Lane ran across one such pocket. Nick's heart sank as they turned into it following the Rolls. It was ill-lit and two cars could pass only with care.

'Christ!' he muttered.

'You can say that again,' the driver said grimly, switching on his headlights.

To add to their concern, the radio operator whose job it was to keep tuned to the device in the container was experiencing difficulty. His frowns and mutterings intensified as he twiddled the knobs in front of him.

A little farther on they saw the brake lights of the Rolls come on and pulled up behind it. Nick jumped out and ran up to the car in front. He noticed the outline of an electric transformer surrounded by a high wire fence on one side of the road and on the other the unmistakable oak.

'I've got a torch,' Nick said quickly to Sir Arnold who had wound down his window.

Stepping across a small ditch he reached the oak and shone his torch into a gash in the trunk near its base. An envelope was propped just inside and he seized it, tearing it open as he skipped back across the ditch.

'Continue for a further two hundred yards along Honey Lane to where a stream runs beside the road. Put the money into the stream and go home. Mr X.'

At that moment another car arrived and Wilcox joined him by the Rolls.

'All right, on we go,' Wilcox said in the tone of a battle commander suddenly haunted by possible flaws in his strategy.

There was no mistaking the place when they got there. A concrete culvert about five feet across and with about three feet of fast flowing water coursing along its man-made channel.

About fifty yards further on Honey Lane reached an end. There was a wire fence across the road and beyond it rose the steep railway embankment.

Where Honey Lane petered out, the stream ran through a tunnel beneath the line.

Wilcox looked at Nick and said something but his words were obliterated by an express train rushing past, the driver of its huge diesel locomotive choosing that moment to add his own comment as he sounded its two tone horn.

As the noise died away, Wilcox said, 'They should be able to catch him on the other side. That's where he'll be waiting. I'll send a message. Meanwhile get the money ready for putting in the water.'

A couple of minutes later, the orange box was lowered into the culvert. As soon as they let go, the current caught it and spun it away.

Nick and another officer ran beside it as far as they could and then watched it disappear into the black opening of the tunnel.

'Why the hell don't we clamber over the top?' the other officer asked.

'First because it's the main line with four tracks and secondly because it wouldn't do us any good anyway.'

'Why do you say that?'

'Because it'll be through to the other side before we're half-way up the embankment this side. Look at the speed that water's flowing and it's even faster in the tunnel because of the constricted space.' He shook his head. 'Mr X has certainly done his homework. So far.'

CHAPTER TWENTY-ONE

It took forty minutes to discover the outlet of the stream on the other side of the railway embankment. Forty minutes during which the ether crackled with instructions, orders, oaths and mounting ill temper.

The trouble was that it continued to flow underground for a further three hundred yards and no-one appeared to know where it emerged. It was just a minor feature on the landscape to which nobody gave any thought. It was *there*.

The local police were unable to help, but tried to get through to the council offices, which were closed. Finally they ran to ground an official in the borough engineer's department who was at home and who gave the answer without even having to swallow his mouthful of supper.

Although the place was not more than a quarter of a mile from where the stream passed into its tunnel beneath the railway, it was nearly three miles of twists and turns by road. And turning the cars in narrow Honey Lane had not made anyone better tempered.

The point at which it did come out into the open was not far from where it joined a disused canal. On one side was the high wall of a now derelict factory and on the other an unkempt cinder path which ended beside the opening of the huge pipe through which the water came flowing out.

Wilcox and Nick stood surveying the scene with despair.

'You can see where somebody's been standing on the edge there,' Wilcox said, shining his torch at the grass which appeared to have been recently trodden down. 'We'll have to go over the whole area for footprints and tyre marks. He must have parked his car at the end of the path, waited here for the money to come floating out and bobs-your-uncle he was off and away.'

'Too bad the bleeper had to pack up at the crucial moment,' Nick remarked.

Wilcox grunted and turned the beam of his torch on the bustling water for a final survey. 'Come on,' he said, 'we're not doing any good hanging around here.'

It was a dispirited party that made its way back to the cars.

As one officer remarked to Nick, 'He didn't even leave us a bloody receipt.'

By the time Wilcox and Nick reached *The Three Ducks*, orders had gone out intensifying the search for Farmer and also notifying police everywhere that Herbert was wanted for questioning.

It was just before eight o'clock when Wilcox gave their driver instructions to park in a side street short of the pub. A couple of minutes later a local C.I.D. officer came up.

'She slipped out about ten minutes ago to make a phone call from the kiosk at the corner of the next block. Otherwise she's been in all the evening, serving in the bar. Is that what you wanted to know, sir?'

'Thanks,' Wilcox said bleakly without enlightening the officer as to the reason for his vigil.

Minnie Dove's look hardened as she saw Wilcox and Nick come into the bar, which had no more than its usual eight to ten customers.

'We'd like a word with you. Upstairs.'

'I can't leave the bar.'

'Where's the lad?'

'In the other bar.'

'Tell him to look after both for a few minutes.'

'Why should I?'

'Go on. Just do as I ask and don't argue.'

Reluctantly she did so and led the way to her sitting-room on the floor above.

There was a tension about her that gave Nick his first feeling of hope that evening.

'What do you want this time?' she asked harshly as soon as they were in the room.

'I'd like to know what you're up to most of all,' Wilcox said.

'Trying to earn an honest living without being harassed by the police.'

'Let's forget the funnies and deal with essentials. Who did you go out and phone just now?'

Her eyes showed surprise for a moment.

'I don't have to answer that and you know it.'

'Why won't you tell me?'

'Because it's none of your business.'

'Why didn't you make the call from here?' Wilcox nodded in the direction of the telephone on the sideboard. When she gave a shrug, he went on, 'Why go out to a public call box when you have a perfectly good telephone at home? Why?'

'I refuse to answer any more questions,' she said in a tone in which anger and agitation were mixed.

'O.K., Mrs Dove, if that really is your answer, so be it. But let me say this. I believe you're in extremely deep water and that shortly I shall have evidence to hang enough charges on you to string along a washing line. And when I do, don't expect me to hold back. If that's clear, we'll now go.'

A nerve twitched at the side of her mouth, but her expression remained utterly hostile.

By nine o'clock they were back at the Yard and in D.A.C. Napier's room.

'Not one of our happier exercises,' the D.A.C. observed, 'though I'm not sure how we could have improved on it. The trouble was that Mr X had planned well and had the initiative throughout. His scheme for collecting the money was a model of ingenuity. Us and him separated by a railway embankment and nearly three miles of winding road.'

'To think he's got right away with £150,000,' Wilcox said in an anguished voice. 'I'm not sure now that we oughtn't to have used paper instead of actual money.'

'And had people filling the emergency wards of hospitals up and down the country?'

'There'd have to have been nationwide publicity warning people not to purchase Swallow Sugar until further notice.'

The D.A.C. pulled a doubtful face.

'You're being wise after the event,' he said. '*If* you're being wise at all. I'm far from convinced. Anyway, there's nothing further we can do tonight save maintain our state of alertness. Ring me at home if there are any developments in the course of the night.'

When Nick reached home around midnight, Clare was reading in bed.

While he undressed, he recounted the day's events culminating in the evening's débâcle.

'Only one person could have thought up such an elaborate plan,' she said when he'd finished. 'Herbert Sipson.'

'And he seems to have got away with it this time,' Nick observed gloomily. 'Though I still don't see how all the bits fit together.'

'Obviously both blackmail schemes have to be seen as part of the same plan,' Clare said thoughtfully.

'The first was as unsuccessful as the second has brilliantly succeeded.'

'Supposing the first wasn't meant to succeed?'

'I'm too tired for riddles, love.'

'Supposing Herbert intended he should be arrested and acquitted?'

'How could he ensure acquittal?'

'By arranging for the demand on Swallow Sugar to take place while he was on trial so that everyone would say that both were the product of the same mind and therefore it must be someone other than Herbert.'

'Too elaborate.'

'But it's succeeded,' Clare said. 'And, anyway, I thought elaborate plans were Herbert's trademark.'

'They've also been his undoing in the past. But not this time.'

'It's too soon to say that.'

'I wish I could think so.'

'It all hangs together,' Clare went on when Nick returned from cleaning his teeth in the bathroom. 'All the blackmail letters typed at the same time some months ago, the coincidence of Herbert's trial and the first demand on Swallow Sugar except, of course, that it's not a coincidence at all. The final instructions for payment not being made until after Herbert's acquittal. His slipping surveillance. Everything fits. He must, of course, have had a co-conspirator. That's where Farmer comes in, perhaps ...'

She paused and waited for Nick's comment. None came, so she glanced down at him. He was asleep.

CHAPTER TWENTY-TWO

Jeffrey Farmer tossed and turned on his none too comfortable bed. He couldn't think why Minnie Dove had not been in touch with him as she had promised.

The previous evening he had spent a whole hour beside the public call box waiting for her call, but it never came. She had told him to be there between half past seven and half past eight and she would ring.

Something must have happened. If she did not make contact with him before noon, he would have to risk phoning her at *The Three Ducks*, despite her warning.

Miss Gunn looked up anxiously as Sir Arnold arrived the next morning.

'Did everything work out all right?' she asked, though his expression told her the answer in advance.

'The chap got away with it,' he said bitterly. 'The whole thing was a fiasco.'

'Well, at least our sugar will be safe.'

Sir Arnold gave a sniff. 'We may have bought time, Miss Gunn, it remains to be seen whether we've bought immunity.' As he passed through the door into his office, he said, 'Please get me Chief Superintendent Wilcox on the phone.'

In fact, Wilcox, who had stayed up all night and had a couple of hours fitful sleep in his office chair, had just gone off for a wash and shave.

When he returned to his office he found a message saying that Sir Arnold had called. Rightly surmising that the chairman of Swallow Sugar was merely phoning to enquire after developments rather than to impart information, Wilcox decided to delay his return call. Indeed, the more he thought about it, the more he realised that Sir Arnold was about the last person on earth he wanted to talk to at that moment. He knew he would have to overcome his inhibition, but at least he would wait until he had breakfast inside him.

When he got back to his office half an hour later, he felt better. He was actively contemplating returning Sir Arnold's call when his extension rang.

'Detective Chief Superintendent Wilcox?' a slightly pedantic voice enquired.

'Yes, Wilcox speaking.'

'My name's Fryer. Registrar-General's Department,' the voice went on. 'I understand you were making enquiries yesterday about a Mr Herbert Sipson?'

'That's right. Have you turned up anything?'

'As a matter of fact we have. I don't know whether it's the man you're interested in, though it's an unusual name. We have a record of a Herbert Sipson getting married at Ealing Register Office on the 16th of August last.'

'Whom did he marry?'

'Yes, you'll want to know that, won't you,' Mr Fryer said in his precise tone. 'Wait a moment, I have it here. Yes, here it is. It was a lady named Minnie Dove. Rather a pretty name, isn't it?'

'It's more than that, Mr Fryer,' Wilcox said enthusiastically. 'It's the most wonderful name you could have mentioned. I'm extremely grateful to you for your help.'

'We've always been happy to co-operate with the police,' Mr Fryer replied primly.

Nick was coming along the corridor when Wilcox dashed from his office.

'Come on,' Wilcox called out. 'We've just had a break. I'll tell you on the way.'

Usually the only sign of activity at a public house at ten o'clock in the morning is clearing up after the previous evening's drinking and some necessary restocking of the bar. When they arrived at *The Three Ducks*, however, there wasn't even this much happening.

The downstairs premises appeared to be deserted. First they rang the bell on the private front door; then, when nobody answered, they thumped on it.

Standing back they gazed up at the first floor windows. Though there was no sign of life, there was equally nothing to arouse any suspicion. The window of the sitting-room was a quarter open.

'It doesn't seem there's anyone at home,' Wilcox observed with a frown. 'We'll go back to the car and wait a few minutes.'

They had scarcely begun to walk away, however, when Minnie Dove herself came hurrying round the corner, her front-door key already in her hand. She came to an abrupt halt when she saw them.

'We're obviously back sooner than you expected,' Wilcox remarked.

'I'm very busy and I've nothing more to say,' she replied with a worried look.

'But we have, Mrs ... Sipson.'

'Oh, my God!' she gasped and put out a hand against the wall to steady herself.

Wilcox took the key from her unresisting hand and opened the door. On reaching the sitting-room he went across to the sideboard and poured her a brandy, which she gulped down in one.

'So you've found that out, have you?' she said with a grimace.

'Where's Herbert?' Wilcox asked.

'Hah! What wouldn't I give to know that!'

'So he's let you down, has he?'

'I've been taken for the longest ride any woman's ever had,' she replied bitterly.

'You'd better tell us. We know you got married last August, how long had you known him?'

'A few months. He used to come here and we got friendly

and he talked about owning a bit of property in the wilds of Canada and I thought he had money. And, anyway, I liked him. And then he suggested that, as we were both on our own, we might think about making a go of things together. So one day we slipped away and got quietly married.' She gave a mirthless laugh. 'It was only afterwards I found out he didn't own a thing, let alone a property in Canada.'

'So he deceived you from the outset?'

She gave a small reflective smile. 'It was kind of mutual, as he only suggested our marrying because he gathered this place was a small goldmine, instead of hocked up to its chimney pots. I told him that about the same time as he told me he didn't have a bean. So there we were spliced and penniless.' She paused. 'As a matter of fact we'd grown quite fond of each other by then. Anyway, he was always full of wonderful schemes for getting hold of money and then one day he comes up with this idea of squeezing the sugar company.'

'How did he pick on them?'

'Because of Farmer. He was always in here grumbling about the way they'd treated him and Herbert said we could use him to our advantage as he was bound to come under suspicion. So we used to encourage him to make phone calls to the company saying how he'd live to see them ruined and all that sort of thing.

'Herbert said he'd work out a plan to end all plans. The only thing was that he was known to the police for his cleverness and they'd immediately suspect him, so there was only one way of ensuring he couldn't be suspected and that was to arrange for himself to be in prison when he asked Swallow Sugar for the money. But he said everything must be prepared in advance before he got himself charged with the first offence.' She shook her head in a bemused manner. 'Sounds daft, doesn't it, telling it like this. But he really believed it would work.'

'It did,' Wilcox remarked quietly.

'The twisting little two-timer.'

'How was he to get in touch with you after collecting the cash last night?'

'He was going to phone me at the call box on the corner at a quarter to eight. If he couldn't get through then for any reason, it was to be at a quarter to nine. If not then, a quarter to ten. And so on.' She let out a harsh noise. 'I spent most of the night running backwards and forwards to that bloody call box.'

'I suppose it was you who posted the letters?'

'Yes.'

'And placed a packet of sugar containing ground glass in the Victoria branch of H.Q. Supermarkets.'

'Yes, but that was the only one.'

'What about the packet sent to Sir Arnold Swallow?'

'Those were the only two. But I didn't have anything to do with preparing them. He left them with me as well as the letters.'

'What about the ones that were going to be put on store shelves if the company didn't pay up?'

'There weren't any more. It was just bluff. I swear it.'

'I hope that's true. It could make a lot of difference to you.'

'I swear it's true. There were just the two packets. There weren't any others.'

'You realise you're up to your neck in this, Minnie?'

'I'm willing to give evidence against him after the way he's treated me,' she said, looking hopefully from Wilcox to Nick.

'You may be willing, but you can't. The law doesn't permit it. You're husband and wife.'

'But I want to.'

Wilcox shook his head impatiently. 'Where's the machine on which the letters were typed?'

'It got thrown away.'

'*Got* thrown away?'

'I threw it away like he told me.'

'How did you know when to start posting the letters?'

'He smuggled out a letter to me from prison. We'd arranged a code.'

'Where's Farmer?'

'At a lodging house in Shepherd's Bush. But he didn't know anything that was going on. He had nothing to do with the plan to get the money. I swear that. After you came here that first time pretending to be insurance men and asking for him, I told him the police were on his track because of his threats to Swallow Sugar and that he'd better clear out. He went to Reading and then Oxford before returning to London.'

'And he kept in touch with you?'

'Yes.'

'And it was because you knew he was in Oxford that you went there to post a couple of the letters?'

'Yes.'

'I can see he had a true friend in you,' Wilcox observed in a scathing tone.

Minnie hung her head. 'There was never any evidence against him. You could never have charged him. He didn't know a thing.'

'We could have arrested him thanks to your use of him.'

'It was all Herbert's idea.'

'But you went along with it very willingly?'

'I was desperate for money.'

'And obviously still are,' Wilcox commented without sympathy. 'You certainly have been left holding an outsize baby. While Herbert skips away with £150,000, you'll be doing five years, at least.'

'Oh, God. No.'

'I don't see what can save you.' He paused. 'Except possibly your help in finding Herbert.'

She shook her head in a despairing manner. 'If I knew where you could lay hands on him, I'd lead you there quicker than you could ask.'

'But you must have had a plan for afterwards?' Wilcox urged.

'He obviously had a plan,' she said viciously. Then, her

spurt of anger quenched, she went on in a tone of weary resignation, 'It was just left that he'd tell me what to do when he phoned.'

A few minutes later, she accompanied the officers to their car and they drove off.

It was on the way that Wilcox suddenly asked, 'How did Herbert manage on his own last night?'

'All he had to do was wait for the cash to float out of that tunnel. We'd rehearsed and timed it so often, he knew exactly how long it would take.' She sighed. 'He was a great one for plans. He always told me that one day he was going to pull off something that would be even greater than the Great Train Robbery because it would be a solo effort, apart from a bit of help from me. Well, it's turned out to be more of a solo effort than I thought he meant.'

And she burst into tears.

CHAPTER TWENTY-THREE

The two men from the borough engineer's department walked up the cinder path which ran beside the stream on the final length of its journey to the canal.

It was a routine, and fairly superficial, inspection of the concrete culvert which they made at infrequent intervals.

They arrived at the point where Herbert, and subsequently the police officers, had stood, leaving the grass edge looking trampled and churned.

'It must 'ave been them police what was 'ere t'other evening,' the taller of the two said, gazing at the scene.

'What was up then?' the shorter one enquired.

'Dunno. Searching for some poor blighter, I 'xpect.'

The shorter man, who was wearing waders, lowered himself cautiously into the water which reached up to his thighs.

He edged his way towards the tunnel exit and, when he got there, bent down and put his head inside the gaping round aperture, through which the water gushed out.

'Give us your torch a minute, Bill,' he said, standing upright again. 'There's a blockage up there.'

'See anything?' the taller one enquired after watching his companion peer for some time into the tunnel.

'Can't see nothing. But there's something holding up back there. I can hear it, I can tell from the sound of the water against it. There's something there all right.'

'Nothing serious anyhow,' the taller one commented. 'Water's getting through all right.'

When they later returned to head office, they mentioned the matter to their inspector.

'We've never had any trouble there before,' the inspector remarked. 'I told the police that the other day. Said it'd take the Q.E.2 to block that channel.'

'Well there's something stuck up there now,' the smaller man said in a definite tone.

The inspector sighed. 'We'd better have a look tomorrow then.'

And so it was that the next morning a man wearing a rubber suit and breathing apparatus made his laborious way into the tunnel while the inspector and the small man stood on the edge and waited.

It was a full fifteen minutes before he blundered out into daylight again. Peeling off his mask, he stared up at the two on the bank with an expression of shock.

'There's a body up there,' he croaked. 'It's a bloke dead.'

The inspector frowned. 'What's holding him?'

'It's about a hundred yards up where there's that bit of a bend. There's a great branch of a tree caught. Pushed up against it by the water is a red box and this bloke's the other side of the box, sort of half on top of it.'

When the box containing the money was recovered, the device was found to be as silent as a bar of soap. The expert answered all criticism, however, by declaring loftily that it had never been designed to transmit from the bowels of the earth and that any earlier signs of failure must have been due to the operator's inexperience. Wilcox realised that the case might be over but the battle of recriminations was only just beginning.

The car which Herbert had used that night was subsequently found concealed in a disused barn beside a track off the end of Honey Lane.

Wilcox and Nick stood in the mortuary gazing at the puffy-faced corpse of Herbert Sipson.

His cause of death, said the pathologist, had been drowning

and his appearance was consistent with his having been in the water for four days.

'When the money didn't come floating out his end,' Nick said, 'he must have waited till we'd all gone and then driven round and entered the tunnel at the Honey Lane end, probably hoping to find it stuck not too far in. I must say I wouldn't have crawled through that tunnel without being properly equipped.'

'Not even for £150,000?'

Nick grinned. 'Well, perhaps.' He turned away from the corpse. 'Poor old Herbert, accident prone to the end!'

POSTSCRIPT

'Minnie Sipson,' Mr Justice Tidyman said severely, 'you have pleaded guilty to a grave offence involving a wicked scheme to blackmail one of the household names in this country. Had the man who conceived that scheme stood beside you in the dock, I should have considered it my public duty to sentence you to a heavy term of imprisonment. But he does not stand beside you because he lost his life in its execution.'

At this point, Minnie brushed away a tear which had begun to fall down her cheek.

'I accept,' the judge went on, 'that you were to a very large extent deceived and duped by that man, who was your husband. I accept what your learned counsel has told me, that you were fond of him and have been deeply affected by his death and that, in the best sense, you remain loyal to his memory despite what has happened. All that is to your credit, as is the fact that you have pleaded guilty today and not sought to contribute your own element of deception to this disgraceful affair. In all these circumstances and, bearing in mind that you have spent the last three months in custody, I have decided that it is just possible not to sentence you to a further custodial term. You will go to prison for two years but the sentence will be suspended for two years. That means you are free to go, but if you commit any other offence during the next two years you will be liable to serve the two years now suspended in addition to any further sentence you receive. Do you understand?'

'Oh, yes, sir,' Minnie exclaimed with a gulp and was led sobbing from the dock.

As they were leaving Court, Wilcox turned to Nick and, with a sardonic smile said, 'Surprising how often justice finally gets done – despite everyone's efforts.'

>>> If you've enjoyed this book and would like to discover more great vintage crime and thriller titles, as well as the most exciting crime and thriller authors writing today, visit: >>>

The Murder Room
Where Criminal Minds Meet

themurderroom.com